Wagon Train West

Center Point
Large Print

Also by Lauran Paine and available from Center Point Large Print:

The Plains of Laramie
Guns in Wyoming
Man from Durango
Prairie Empire
Sheriff of Hangtown
Rough Justice
Gunman's Moon
Wyoming Trails
Kansas Kid
Trail of Shadows

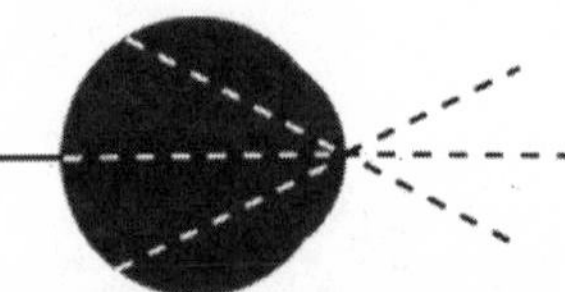

Wagon Train West

Lauran Paine

CENTER POINT LARGE PRINT
THORNDIKE, MAINE

This Circle Ⓥ Western is published by
Center Point Large Print in the year 2016 in
co-operation with Golden West Literary Agency.

First Edition
April, 2016

Printed in the United States of America
on permanent paper.
Set in 16-point Times New Roman type.

ISBN: 978-1-62899-942-6

Library of Congress Cataloging-in-Publication Data

Names: Paine, Lauran, author.
Title: Wagon train west : a Circle V western / Lauran Paine.
Description: First edition. | Thorndike, Maine : Center Point Large Print, 2016. | ©2016
Identifiers: LCCN 2015045178 | ISBN 9781628999426
(hardcover : alk. paper)
Subjects: LCSH: Large type books. | GSAFD: Western stories.
Classification: LCC PS3566.A34 W34 2016 | DDC 813/.54—dc23
LC record available at http://lccn.loc.gov/2015045178

Chapter One

With the wind sighing like a lost thing, low against the tall spring grass, there was no other sound. In a vastness of space and a vacuum of silence there was no movement for a long while, then, when movement came, it was a horse impatiently bobbing his head.

Just that quick, fretting motion and no more. The shifting pattern made by the hugging wind through the grass was like the gray, passing shadow of a giant, stalking southward.

In all that immense, gigantic wilderness, there was little to mark the passage of man. The giant, buttressed mountains far off were splashed over with the sun's bold strokes. The land fall that ran out to meet a vaguely hazed horizon was vast beyond reckoning. Yet the only thing that moved in all this was simply the impatience of a horse.

Slowly, sitting there alone on a jagged crusting of rock, the Dakota's head moved just the smallest bit. Motionless in the dawn light of the forest's fringe was the warrior sentinel. Back, where the new warmth made soft shadows, was his horse.

The moon still hung, white and sharp, in the pinkening sky and the gray color of first dawn was gone. The Eagle's Nest was a gleaming tower of blood under the reddening light and, north of the warrior, Stone Face loomed, dark and brooding like the face of God. The little spring wind whipped raw at his body, a speck in the vastness. There was only eternal time, poised and hushed, and a silent cry vivid in the warrior's mind like flaming triumph. *Wagon train!*

As still as Stone Face, as brooding and inward and majestic, the big man of war moved his head again a fraction, following the course of a lone horseman. He watched with glistening, wet, black eyes the solitary figure, no larger than an ant, riding slowly, tiredly back toward the wagon circle, from a scout up the gently rolling land north of where the emigrants had made their nightly bivouac. The warrior rose up slowly from the rock and turned a little to watch the white man swing over to the circle of huge, clumsy wagons. Looking farther out, northward, he knew other spies like himself were there, watching. The Dakotas had been following this wagon train for two days now. From a dozen places of concealment they kept a silent, grim watch.

The white people were holding to a swale of land that wound its way between craggy upthrusts and smooth mountains whose ageless faces loomed, immense in the soft glow. They were trespassing across Indian country. It was Dakota Indian country at that; the domain of powerful and war-like stalwarts the whites called the Sioux.

This was 1864. The entire breadth of the plains was afire. No man was safe, be he white, Dakota, Northern Cheyenne, half-breed, or emigrant passing through, tooling his big wagon westward toward the setting sun. The Civil War far off in the white man's country had drained away the soldiers. The Plains Indians were embarked upon the last and final effort they would make to throw back the tide of empire. There was no peace anywhere and the black-gray mountains of this grimly silent land echoed with the screams of the aroused *ozuye we' tawatas*—the men of war—the Dakota and Northern Cheyenne fighting warriors.

And down in the rough circle of the wagons where the smell of animals was strong and the faces of people were pinched tight with tension, drawn like the warhead of an Indian drum, Kit Butler swung off his horse and gazed from level blue eyes at the turmoil of men walking, women cooking the morning meal, and children in a fecundity of hushed irresolution, wandering everywhere. One hundred and sixty people—seventy-seven were men. His lean body stood beside the tired horse. A small boy came and took the reins and led the animal away.

He stood so still that Lige Turner, poking at a sickly fire, stopped what he was doing to look at him. But for the low breeze that rippled Kit's blond hair, he would have looked like a carving. His slimness with its aura of indefatigable strength was projected vividly against the massiveness of the old, scarred wagons. His waist was circled by a brass-studded cartridge belt from which carelessly hung a Colt Dragoon pistol. He held a carbine, butt down, with his right hand, showing the easy familiarity of a man who had never been out of reach of guns. His face was deeply etched from experiences blasted out of a stark existence, and yet he wasn't more than twenty-five or thirty years of age. His chest was broad and deep, his belly ribbed with tawny muscle, and something about him set him apart from the drabness of the people who had hired him and Lige to pilot them across the Indian country—something wild and savage and brutal, like the land, and hushed and inward, too.

Lige, who had seen the expression many times, watched the play of brooding gravity over the sharply chiseled, bronzed face. It was like a far-off storm first appearing over the rim of the horizon, spreading lowering shadows threateningly downward, over the lower portion of Kit's face. He sighed and poked glumly at the snapping little flames of a breakfast fire.

He recalled their rough existence back at Independence, on the Missouri, with a mountain man's nostalgia. Those were the days when men stood on their own feet or were carried out by them. The fur trade was gone, thanks to Europe's importation of new styles based on silk and chintz and what-not. The trappers were scattered or piloting people like these—emigrants with long beards, subdued homespun clothing, and unwieldy, inaccurate guns. Many a night he and Kit Butler had squatted at an Indian powwow and gorged on half-cooked buffalo hump, had joined in the violent and unrestrained dancing, had drunk the Dakotas and Arapahoes, the Rees and Cheyennes and Shoshones under the table, then laid down among them and slept like babes.

Not any more. A few whites of mountain man caliber had been all right—even welcomed among them. This was different. These psalm-singing emigrants who came now killed game without need, fired forests to clear paths for their wagons, and burned off prairie grass to make it hard for Indian horses to graze near the trails. Times had changed.

Shaking his head, Lige looked around again and called softly: "Kit, come eat." He watched the scout move toward him and sighed again. Kit used the same long springing stride, as though he still wore moccasins instead of the foot-killing cowhide boots. The same blunt jaw set, like the prow of a ship, jutted out to meet life head-on. "Well, what did you find?"

Kit dropped down and folded his legs. He gazed into the fire with his sharp look and shrugged. "What you'd expect, I reckon."

"Indians?"

"Indian sign. Dakotas. They've been trailing us for a couple of days."

"Many of the devils?"

"Enough," Kit said succinctly. "We're pretty deep into their country now."

Lige hung a limp piece of red meat between two forked sticks and held the morsel over the fire, turning it from time to time with a solemn watchfulness. "Northern Cheyennes with 'em?"

"Doesn't look like it. Looks to me like just Dakotas . . . but a big band of them. Maybe a hundred."

Lige swore softly and turned the meat. The smell rose and swirled around them when the breeze came warmly. "We're in for a skittle then, I'd say. Do these *wasichus* know it?"

Kit shook his head. "Naw, what the hell . . . they send out five or six men and ride all over the tracks. They sit on their horses, shading their cussed eyes and look out over the country. It's funny."

"It would be," Lige agreed, "if it wasn't so danged pathetic."

Kit took the meat Lige offered and started to eat. "You can tell them ten times in a row to look down . . . that Indian signs are on the ground, not ten miles away, but they wouldn't know a Dakota moccasin print from a buffalo's track." He chewed slowly. "Funny thing about these people. They expect to see Indians charging in a big band, like soldiers, straight at them."

Lige began cooking another piece of meat. "I know," he said dryly. "Hell, in the old days they wouldn't have lasted a week out here."

Kit raised his glance and watched a big, thick man with a black spade beard approaching. He spoke softly to Lige. "Here comes Powers."

Lige tested his meat without heeding the wagon boss who gazed down at them from his broad, flat face with small, cold eyes. He squatted heavily, grunting like a sow.

"Well, what'd you find?"

"Indians," Kit said. "Dakotas. Looks like a pretty big band. I figure they've got us surrounded by now."

"Indians!" Powers said explosively, derisively. "I haven't seen one since we come out of Independence. Everybody talks Indians. It's like a disease with you fellers."

Lige began to eat. He chewed his meat with short, savage strokes and his eyes were unpleasant. But he said nothing and looked steadily at the trodden earth across the cooking fire from where they sat.

Kit watched the big emigrant's face work with scorn in a wry and thoughtful way. "Might be at that," he said calmly. "Tell you what, Powers." He lifted an arm and pointed toward the towering cliff south, where the big Dakota had been earlier. "Send one of your boys over to the base of that hill and have him look around for moccasin tracks. If he doesn't find some, I'll finish scouting for you to Fort Collins without any pay."

Lige looked up, shocked. At thirty-five he looked fifty, the way the morning sun caught his face and shone off it. Powers's eyes misted for a second of indecision, then they cleared and he struck his leg. "You heard, Turner. You're witness." He got up ponderously and stalked away without a word. Lige gulped his last mouthful and looked pained. Kit smiled in the wolf-fierce way he had.

"He'll have to pay me, don't worry. I made that circuit before daybreak. There's one on top of the hill, up there by the forest's edge. I found where he walked around leading his horse, hunting for a trail up."

Lige swung and squinted at the abrupt, craggy rampart, then his glance fell to where several emigrant men were standing beside a reckless-eyed youth on a big sorrel horse. He grunted and squirmed to watch. "They're sending out that red-headed hellion, the one that's always hunting a fight."

Kit watched the rider wind his way out of the wagon circle and make steadily toward the cliff. His eyes were slitted speculatively. There was no reason to think the Dakota was still up there, except that, in the gray light hours before, he hadn't found any tracks coming down. He waited.

The rumor of his wager with the wagon boss

went around. People talked and watched. "Well," Kit said, "it gets their minds off hardship anyway."

"Hardship?" Lige snorted. "They don't know what hardship is. Look at them wagons. By God, they even carry water casks with 'em. There's not a one that's ever gone two days with his tongue thickening. Hardship! *Owgh!*"

"They think they're suffering now," Kit said, watching the rider grow small. There was a hard, bright edge to his words. "They'll find out before we get to Fort Collins, I think. Those Dakotas'll hit us one of these dawns. They aren't trailing us for company."

"Where d'you reckon they picked us up?"

"Hard to say now, Lige. Thirty wagons throw up one hell of a dust banner this time of the year. Anyway, they're all on the warpath now, from Mexico to Canada. They'll have scouts out all over the cussed country. You know how it is in the spring. They need horses to replace the ones that've starved, and they're hungry and restless, like wolves. This is going to be a bad year. The sign is out already."

Lige sucked his teeth in suppressed anxiety. The wages Kit had bet were important to them. He tugged his old hat low over his eyes and watched the rider approach the cliff. People were standing as if they were rooted. Even children watched, not understanding perhaps but catching some of the contagion from their elders.

Then the red-headed emigrant dismounted and walked, leading his horse. He was clearly following a track of some kind. A soft murmur went up from the watching people. Lige looked over at Kit with a relieved, hard smile. "You should've bet Powers for money," he said. He was still looking at Kit's dark profile when the rending shout went up from the watchers. With an oath he swung for another look, Kit's growl rumbling close by as the younger man sprang up, clawed at his rifle, and began to trot toward the southernmost wagon.

Lige followed, wondering, feeling the way his stomach tightened into a knot of gristle. The emigrants were motionless and only the horror in their cries made a second look necessary. Kit elbowed through them, twisting and hurrying. Lige trailed in his wake.

The drama was ending when Kit could see without the impairment of hats and heads. The red-headed boy was being held close beside the racing horse of a brilliantly arrayed Dakota man of war. His feet threshed in a crazy dance and the Indian had him powerfully by the hair. He was scalping the white man without slowing his horse, dragging him so that dust arose in their wake. Then, with a contemptuous movement, the Dakota flung the body aside and let out a yell that carried as clear as the wail of a bull elk, down to the wagon train. He was holding aloft a fiery tuft of hair. The sun shone brilliantly off it.

Kit didn't wait. He fought his way clear of the press of sickened people and raced for his horse. Lige was less than ten feet behind him. There was only the delay to bridle. Bareback, they raced neck and neck toward the big Dakota. With a swift, sign-language gesture of contempt, he lowered his trophy and sped easily away from the pursuit.

Kit slowed his horse and rode at a jolting trot where the red-headed emigrant lay. He was dead. The warrior's last knifing slash had split his gullet from ear to ear. Lige stayed on his horse, steady-eyed and watchful, while Kit kneeled by the body. Neither of them spoke for a moment, then Kit stood up, dusted his knees, and looked after the Dakota. He was gone. Kit turned toward the wagon circle and gazed for a long time at it, then he stooped, hefted the body, tossed it across his horse, and leaped up behind it. Still in silence they turned back. The emigrants were moving frantically. Kit watched their senseless activity with an inward darkness of the spirit.

"Maybe they'll believe now, Lige."

"Hell of a way to find out," Lige said dourly. "Still, if it had to be someone, I reckon this one's the best. He was a cussed bully anyway."

"They don't look at things like that, Lige. Any white man, even a worthless one, is better'n fifty Indians to them."

"*Owgh*!" Lige was watching the streaming

people coming afoot out to meet them. "Now'd be the time for the bucks to raise the yell. Look at 'em. I'll bet they're not twenty left inside the circle."

Kit shrugged. "We're in for bad trouble with this batch, I know. Too late to go back . . . they wouldn't anyway, with Powers as their leader . . . and hell to pay if we go ahead. In Shoshone country this would be bad enough, but here, with Dakotas around us, we're likely not to get even to Fort Collins."

Their horses were engulfed in a torrent of upturned, horrified faces. Hands clawed at the dead man's body. Kit released his hold and watched the way the scalpless man was whisked away amid the first discordant notes of wailing. Someone rapped his knee with a hard fist. It was Powers. The man's face was shiny with sweat, and ugly.

"I want to talk to you."

"Come on, then," Kit said, riding through the people, back toward the breakfast that had been interrupted. Lige took the horses and left Kit with the wagon boss. They squatted where the dying fire was. Powers looked dogged and gray under his flat-brimmed hat with its sweat-marked, low crown.

"I don't like the looks of it, Butler. They must be trailing us like coyotes. That was a terrible thing. The people'll be hard to handle now. They were scairt enough before."

"You weren't?" Kit said flatly.

Powers flagged impatiently with one big hand. "I was, maybe, and didn't know it. It's the danged Indian talk all the time. A man gets so full of it he's like to burst."

Kit didn't help Powers. He sat there without speaking, looking past the wagon boss where the emigrants were talking in groups; the women were crowding around one wagon where a gray-faced man stood like stone, unseeing, looking past them all, and where the sounds of anguish came whimperingly from within the big canvas top.

He thought of how this same black-bearded man had come swaggering into the little camp he and Lige had made, back on the Missouri a few miles below Independence, seeking scouts in a lofty, patronizing way. He hadn't liked Powers then and didn't like him now. He sat in the warmth, waiting for the wagon boss to go on speaking, refusing to help him with word or gesture even though he understood well enough the sudden fear that was growing, haunting, the emigrant leader.

"Well," Powers said finally, looking up at Kit. "What shall we do?"

"You're the wagon boss, not me."

"I'm asking for your suggestions."

Kit was watching the emigrant men congregate around the stony-eyed father of the red-headed youth. He could tell a lot from the way they stood, clutching their guns with white knuckled fists and speaking in low, vibrant tones. He shrugged. "Make soldiers out of those people. Live like the Indians live. They've found out from hundreds of years in this country that there's only one way to survive. Make fighters of your men and workers of your women."

"How?" Powers asked dully. "These people aren't Indians. They're farmers."

Kit's eyes glowed with a steady, bright intentness. "Listen, Powers. In country like this you work *with* Nature . . . you don't change her. If it takes fighting and working to stay alive, then you fight and work, or you don't stay alive. It's damned simple. You get these people around your council fire and tell them what's got to be done. They either do it or they don't. If they don't . . ." Kit made a knife-slashing gesture over his throat. It was a ruthless reminder of what had happened to the dead man.

Powers sat slumped. He was lost in thought. He didn't look up when Lige joined them and hunkered closely beside Kit and spoke Dakota in a low tone.

"Kit, they're going to make trouble. They've been talking. They say we could have prevented that killing. They even say we might be working with the Indians."

Kit listened in silence. He raised his head and cast another long look at the restless emigrant men who were gazing at them now with faces twisted and ugly. He looked beyond them to the towering escarpment where the Dakota had waylaid the youth. Up above where the pine forest lay, a gray, oily mist was rising from the warming earth, hovering over the purple darkness of the endless trees like a fallen bit of sky. The presence of disaster and tragedy was in the dazzlingly clear air with its shimmering distances made magically close. All the trouble didn't lie beyond the ragged circle of thirty Conestogas; it was here as well. Behind Powers, walking now, at least fifty men strode toward them with cruel, vengeful, tensed faces.

The knot of men came unsteadily, but they came. Kit uncoiled his legs and stood up. He was close beside the shorter, broader figure of Lige Turner. Powers looked up quickly, read their faces, and got up clumsily with a low sound in his throat like a threatening mastiff. He turned when the emigrant men stopped a scant five feet away.

"What's the meaning of this?"

The dead man's father, his lips a blue, bloodless line and his eyes like old ashes wet with dark rain, stared, unseeing, past the wagon boss at Kit and Lige. "Those men . . . they done that a-purpose. We want 'em." There was a strong, deep ringing to the voice.

Kit's voice was a two-edged knife when he spoke. "I didn't know that would happen. No one could have foreseen that. Listen to me. You've been told for five weeks now that you were going into Sioux country. You've been told what would happen if you didn't keep vigilance all the time. Well, you're far enough from help now so the Dakotas can hit you. From now on your lives won't be worth any more than that fellow's life was, if you don't form up a fighting force of your own and keep a watch as sharp as an Indian would."

"You two scoundrels are with the heathen!" a fiery-faced hot-eyed man said, taking a resolute step forward.

Lige made a trilling, Indian sound of warning. Kit could sense the older man's bunching of muscle. He put a hand out and touched Lige's arm. "Hold it," he said, then he stared at the emigrant who had spoken. His voice was soft and ironic.

"Only a damned fool would say a thing like that. Do you think the Dakotas, or Sioux as you call 'em, would choose between one white man's scalp and another? If you do, you're pretty damned ignorant about Indians. They wouldn't, not now. They're fighting a war against *all* white men. You know that, too. You heard it at Independence, and all along the trail, every time we passed other trains."

The gray-faced man was beyond reason. He had cause to be. The sight of his son, hairless, his throat a gaping scarlet hole, left him with but one vivid thought frozen into his stunned mind . . .

death. He gathered himself and rocked forward on his toes. Lige caught the slight movement easily, and Kit did, too. He spoke with an icy hardness to his words.

"I reckon, boys, you're set on trouble. I'd sort of like that, maybe." His hand was resting like a talon on his pistol butt. He went on evenly and clearly. "You're worse than a herd of fools. Well, it'd sort of please me to blow a few of your gutless bellies past your backbones. I never had much patience with men who wouldn't learn out here. Go ahead . . . make your rush. We'll go to hell together."

"A lot of us," Lige said, smiling. "The ones Kit leaves I'll salivate. Come on, you cussed lard bellies. What we leave the damned Indians can have. When they get through with you, you'll wish to hell we'd done it with bullets."

The men stopped as though they had run against a wall. They shuffled their feet. None of the unpleasantness had gone out of their faces, though. They were just uncertain, lacking leadership. Powers stood, wide-legged, facing them. He hadn't said a word. Now he did, his bull-bass voice rumbling with strong passion.

"Don't think this'll help us any, you fools? Whatever you think of these men, we need 'em. I'm convinced they know their trade."

The red-faced man spoke swiftly, bitterly. "So do their friends, the Injuns," he said.

Powers looked down at the emigrant with a flash of fury. “Shut your mouth, Reaves, or I’ll let you do the scouting.”

Powers saw the short man’s suddenly pale look. He smiled cruelly. “Fact is . . . from now on you go out with Turner and Butler every time they ride, damn you. If you find they’re meeting Injuns out there, you can come back and tell us. After that, we’ll know how to deal with ’em.” He looked at the other men. Their first rush of blood was cooling. It showed in their faces and in the bewildered, worried look in their eyes. “Any of the rest of you want to be scouts, too?” He gave them no chance to answer. He had the advantage and knew it. He pushed on relentlessly. “As long as I’m wagon boss, we’ll have no mutinies. We’re bad off . . . Kit’ll tell you that. We’ve got to hang together.”

When Powers stopped speaking, the silence was oppressive. Kit hooked his thumbs in the gun belt around his middle and watched the faces. He smiled in a thin, contemptuous way. It was the first time he had ever heard Powers use his given name. It was significant. He looked around at Lige and was surprised to see Lige’s big pistol out and cocked, belly-high. Speaking low, he told Lige to holster it. The old mountain man looked murderous. He put up the gun, though, and relaxed a little.

Kit faced the emigrants. “Powers and I have

talked. I want the best fifty men among you to make into a war party." He was aware of the wagon boss' questioning glance and ignored it. "You're going to have to fight, and it won't be long. I want to whip us up a little army of our own. We don't want anyone who's too Dutch-headed to learn and obey orders. We want the best riflemen among you and the best riders. If you'll work with Lige and me in this, I think you'll more'n likely make it through to Fort Collins. If not . . . I don't know."

"Just how cussed strong *are* these Indians, anyway?" a man asked in a complaining, garrulous way.

"Banded together, they could mount a thousand warriors and more. By individual bands and war parties, I reckon they'd have no trouble mustering a hundred or two hundred men of war."

A stunned silence settled. The murderous mood was broken by Kit's words. He drew grim satisfaction from their worried faces.

"There's another thing. We're in a circle here. They don't like to fight sieges or ride against men who are behind bulwarks. They're out there, waiting. Now, you can break your circle and head out, or you can stay here and wait."

Powers was looking at Kit intently. He appeared very worried. "But hell, we das'n't stay here. We've got to make time."

Kit shrugged. "Then strike camp and string 'em

out. But if you do, make up a war party of your own, because I'll lay you a bet they're waiting for you to break the circle."

"You think they'll attack when we're all strung out?"

"I do." Kit turned to Lige. "What d'you say, pardner?" Lige didn't speak. He just nodded his head in a bleak and moribund way that was very eloquent.

The emigrants spoke in low tones among themselves. It was as though at least half of them were embarrassed over their behavior. Others said nothing, keeping hard and suspicious stares on the two scouts. Powers bent to listen to a skinny, angular man with a great, long, hickory-stocked Pennsylvania rifle that reached to his shoulder. Kit let his breath out softly, so it would make no sound, and his inner feeling of contempt for these farmers was leavened a little with a hard sort of pity. They were like sheep, like children lost in a great forest, hating the trees and wanting to fight them without seeing it was hopeless.

Lige tugged at his elbow. "Have 'em pool their powder and ball, then divvy it up."

Powers turned with a dark, resolute look. "We'll string 'em out," he said. "The men are willing for you to choose among 'em who you reckon'll be best for the war party." He turned with a self-conscious frown and waved a thick arm. "Spread out, boys. Get in lines so's Kit can see you."

Kit made the interview brief. He asked the same questions of every man he sized up as promising. "Is your horse strong? Have you plenty of bullets? Is there someone else who can tool your wagon?"

Those who answered affirmatively he sent after their bullets and horses. The rest he dismissed without a word, then he went over where the wagon boss and Lige were standing. Powers looked forbidding. His small eyes were grimly fixed on the dragging steps and drooping head of the dead youth's father. He shook himself slightly when Kit spoke.

"Don't break up the circle until I've got riders out."

For a moment Powers said nothing, then he looked up into Kit's face. "Are you sure? It's hard to believe they'd attack a train of thirty wagons."

Lige was leaning on his rifle, chewing tobacco. He spat with a sharp, explosive sound. "Sure? You can't be sure of nothing here. I'll tell you this, though. The good Lord's been protecting all of us this far. They could've struck any time, up to now."

"At night," Powers said, with fear and dread thick in the words.

"No, Dakotas hardly ever fight at night. Oh, a few rambunctious young bucks might try a coup or two, but no Dakota war party'll hit you at night. They don't believe a man ought to get killed in the dark. They think he'll have to stumble around in the dark all the rest of eternity and be unable to find his way to the Sand Hills."

"Sand Hills?" Powers repeated questioningly.

"Their heaven," Kit said. "They call it *Odi Maka Cantewaste.* Means Happy Hunting Ground, or the Great Sand Hills."

The three of them stood watching the activity, none speaking. The emigrants were striking camp. Women and children were stowing iron pots and steel tripods into the big wagons. There was a bustle of motion that stirred up dust. It hung in the air with a hot, acrid odor. Men fumbled at horse and oxen harness, big oaken neck yokes, and chain tugs, sweat-stiff bellybands and britchings. Some dogs, lean and sly-eyed, ran among the confusion.

Someone called out sharply to Powers. He walked away, leaving the scouts alone in their watchful, slouching stance. Lige spat again and shook his head like a wounded buffalo bull.

"Like children," he said softly. "Like danged children. Look, here comes your army. Well, they look better on a horse anyway." He straightened up as Kit watched the straggling riders cross the wagon circle. "I'll fetch our critters."

Kit's eyes flickered appraisingly over the men. There were over fifty of them, closer to sixty-five. They carried every manner of gun from large bore buffalo rifles to the slim, almost fragile-looking Kentucky and Pennsylvania muskets. The division was about equal between muzzleloaders and breechloaders. Some men had pistols jammed into their waistbands while others had shell belts around them. Almost all of them had Bowie knives. Well, it could be worse. If they'd fight at all, the Indians might get a bellyful.

He didn't speak to any of them until Lige came back with their horses. He mounted and leaned on the flat Texas horn of his A-fork saddle. "This is how the Indians do it," he said, "and we're going to do it the same way. Lige'll take half of you and ride on one side of the wagons. I'll take the other half and ride on the opposite side. We'll detail about ten men to ride behind the train and send about five to ride up ahead, strung out, so the word can be passed quickly back if the farthest scout sees anything." He paused, waiting for questions, his eyes roaming over their faces.

"Now then, if anything happens too fast for you to send back word, or if you've got to signal for anything, shoot into the air once. Aside from that there's to be no shooting at all. And remember this. If one of you goes to sleep on the march, you can be responsible for the scalping . . . and worse . . . of every person in this train." He swung toward Lige and rolled his head sideways toward the emigrant men. "Pick what you want, Lige. I'll be back in a minute."

He rode carefully through the turmoil until he found the wagon boss. "You ready to roll them, Powers?"

"Whenever you think we ought to."

Kit nodded curtly. "The only thing that'll make your farmers into fighters now is experience. They're ready and so am I. String 'em out when you want."

He reined back and rode to where Lige had divided the mounted men. He could hear Lige laying into them in a hard, flat tone that was almost snarling with its suppressed hostility. He smiled to himself. Lige was like an Indian; he rarely forgave and never forgot.

Chapter Two

The sound rose of drovers calling to their teams and spans. With it went the thicker, sturdier sounds of the great wagons creaking out of the protective circle. Horses whinnied and oxen lowed. Men shouted encouragement to their beasts and one another and the thick dust churned beneath the steel tires.

Kit waved to Lige and beckoned to the riders who were a little apart, waiting. They filed out of the broken circle on opposite sides. Kit rode clear of the stinging dust with its strong smells and swung leisurely westward, watching the train form into a long, spaced serpentine with the loose stock driven a little to one side and to the rear.

The sounds gradually settled into a dirge of constancy, made up of many small complaints from wheels and creaking tailgates, from the rattling clank of chain tugs to the fluted echoes of men with long goad poles, yelling to their animals.

Lige, north of the train, waved his hat. Kit waved back, then ran a hard glance over the men closest to him. He called three out and sent them up ahead of the train. They were the frontal scouts—the feelers. Lige sent three more. Kit watched them loping in a swinging arc until they came together, then he sat there watching to see if they would do as he had told them. They did. Two stayed back in front of the lead wagon and the others strung out farther afield and ahead. He felt satisfied so far, but it didn't show in his face.

The land stretched new and clear as a diamond around them. There was no trail. Where the big wheels ground into the earth, they were marking out twin ruts that would remain to guide others long after their passing was a memory. Following the long valleys, they hoped to avoid the narrow passes and the forests where immense trees, as closely packed as hairs on the head, would balk them.

Kit knew this country, but in a general way—in the way that a man on a horse would know it. To a mounted man it offered no serious obstacle. To these grinding behemoths with their hind wheels taller than a man afoot, it offered a hundred insurmountable obstacles: forests, cliffs, spring-swollen rivers, and uncharted miles of sameness where the grass was stirrup high to a mounted man. And Dakotas—men like White-Shield-Owner and High-Back-Bone—these were called "hump" warriors and they were as fierce and courageous, as brutal and clever as any white man who would meet them. They were fanatics like There-Is-A-Burning-Sky and Big Eagle (he of the perpetual squint and weak, failing eyesight).

Kit thought of the times he had laughed and

hunted with Dakotas, of the times he had hidden, in dread, from them. Of all the things he had ever done, what he was doing now was the most foolhardy. At least, in the trapping days, when the Indians had been stirred up, the mountain men had discreetly laid low and waited it out. Not anymore.

Emigrants came streaming endlessly. They choked the trails and dammed up the highways with their wagons and herds. They overran the frontier settlements and burst out like blind mice, tooling westward into the face of—they didn't know what. It was a crazy, irrational thing, but they did it, and those who hung back shook their heads. When the tales of disaster and blood-curdling tragedy came filtering back, there were always legions who nodded and said: "I knew it'd happen. I told you so, consarn 'em, the idjits."

Kit thought the things he had often thought and kept his eyes, like an Indian's, far-roving, never still, prying and suspicious and always moving. The hours went by and the sun hesitated overhead. Powers rode out to him and reined in alongside. His face was oily with sweat, his eyes troubled under the low brim of his hat.

"Dast we stop for nooning?"

Kit shook his head. It pleased him a little, too. As Lige had said, these people didn't know what hardship really was. "No." Just that and no more. He might have been on the verge of saying more.

Instead of speaking, though, he stiffened suddenly.

From one of the coves that led into the shadowy gloom of the forested slope westward riders were coming. They were a long way off, possibly a mile, but no one who had trained himself, so that even in sleep he was inwardly coiled like a tight spring, would ever mistake identifying them—Dakotas!

"Powers, alert the people," he said softly. Then he reined away and rode up beside a tall, gaunt man with a flinty look in his weathered face. "Ride around to the other party. Tell them there are Sioux up ahead. *Ride, dammit!*"

In shock the emigrant shot a startled glance at Kit's face. He saw enough although he hadn't seen any Indians. He rode swiftly, making an ungainly caricature on a big horse. Kit went back over to where Powers was squinting, leaning forward a little in his anxiety. The wagon boss' hand was white where it held the saddle horn, gripping the leather-covered wood. Kit stared hard at the distant, vague images pouring down across their path far ahead. He saw the forward scouts reel back and break over into a headlong race back toward the wagons. They seemed to move with maddening slowness. He wondered that the Indians hadn't fired on the scouts. There was something contemptuous in the silent way they filed down across the trail ahead.

Kit's mouth hardened beneath the slanting shade

of his hat brim. "Dammit, Powers, go warn your people!"

Suddenly he felt the bone-crushing grip of the older man on his arm. Startled, he half turned. Powers's face was twisted with an expression of fascination and dread. He released Kit's arm and pointed wordlessly, staring. Kit swore at him. Then Powers overcame his alarm and wheeled away, spurring his horse needlessly. Kit sat back then, staring coldly at the streaming men of war, a tumult of fierce satisfaction hammering through his veins. *Now* they'd find out whether frontiersmen thought they saw or smelled Indians where there weren't any.

Lige came riding like the wind. He cut flashingly between two wagons, ignoring the indignant shouts of the drovers, and slammed his horse into a sliding halt beside Kit.

"Did you tell 'em to corral?"

"Not yet. They're up to something, Lige. If it was simply to fight, they'd've hit us hard before this."

Lige's eyes narrowed, looking at the far distant horsemen. His jaw muscles rippled excitedly. Riders careening down the length of the train diverted his attention for a moment. He smiled savagely, gloatingly.

"*Owgh*! Now they're getting scairt to death, Kit. Look at 'em."

Kit did. He saw several men loping toward him. Powers was in the lead. He growled in annoyance:

"They go from one extreme to the other, Lige. Better get back over to your lads. I'll have Powers corral the wagons pretty quick."

Lige was reluctant. "Pass me word of what's up, Kit."

Kit nodded, and Lige trotted back the way he had come. The swirl of riders brought dust with them. Kit looked at Powers when the wagon boss was close. "You'd best corral 'em now, I reckon." He said it quietly and several of the emigrant men drew a thin measure of confidence from his calmness. Powers sent a man back with the order, then faced Kit again.

"The forward scouts say there're a hundred of 'em."

Kit looked back. The Indians, closer now, were unmoving, presenting a long single rank of warriors blocking the progress of the train. They stretched from the forest on one side of the long, narrow valley to the trees on the other side. There were at least a hundred of them. He squinted, riding slowly with the emigrants on both sides of him, silent and watchful.

Powers spoke in a charged, sharp way. "A hundred guns! Lord!"

"Damn their guns," Kit snorted. "They're lined out like that to tell you that you can't go a step farther across Dakota territory. You're lucky. There must be a wise head among 'em. They're being made to warn you first . . . fight you second.

Well, what'll I tell 'em? You're going on or turning back?"

The men said nothing. Kit turned irritably toward the wagon boss, scowling. "Well?"

"We've got to go on, Kit," Powers said in a subdued, strained voice.

Kit looked at the other men. They were just as awed and just as determined as Powers was. He drew in a deep breath that was like bitter-root in his throat.

"Then you're going to have one hell of a fight with them. Mark that down and remember it."

They continued to ride after the train had stopped. The thin voices of women and children came softly over the valley to them from the wagons. Kit swung for a look at Lige's men. They were converging as he and his party were, toward the front of the inward-swinging lead wagon. There was need now for cessation of thinking. From now on he would have to move and speak like an Indian, with instinct and native shrewdness, with wile and diplomacy and eloquent gestures, for no Indian used words where sign language served better. He knew their ways well. Once the war leader, Hump, had said: "In all this land there is no white man whose blood is like our blood . . . but Ohiyesa."

Kit thought back to that with a cold smile. Ohiyesa—The Winner—his Dakota name. Time would tell whether he was a winner or not.

Chapter Three

The Dakotas were startling, the way the golden sun struck the line of motionless horsemen. Kit reined up when the two groups, his and Lige's, converged like a spearhead where the front wagon had been. Powers sat erect, just looking. Lige was moving his jaws rhythmically, his leathery face riveted on the nearest Indian.

Kit studied the symbols, the zigzag marks on faces, the drawings daubed brilliantly on horses, the tall coup sticks and lances. "Ogallalas," he said aloud to no one in particular. "The fightingest Dakotas there are. God damn!"

As though brought back to the present by Kit's blasphemy, the wagon boss spoke without looking around. "There's a lot of them," he said needlessly.

Lige grunted. It was a habit he had acquired from these same Indians. "Kit, look there. The old fellow riding toward us."

Kit watched three men detach themselves from the long rank of barbaric warriors and ride forward at a walk. He also heard Powers say something under his breath and turned. "You stay here. Send a man back to the wagons with orders for no one to make a hostile move, then you stay up here and watch. Keep the boys here pacified.

One wrong move and all hell's going to bust loose. Come on, Lige."

He rode as slowly as the Dakotas were doing, with as much dignity as he could summon. His mind was dark with unbidden thoughts, for if the emigrants wouldn't turn back and the Dakotas refused to let them go on—there was going to be war.

The Indians stopped and only one kept coming. He wasn't a tall, bronzed warrior. Instead, he was a small, stocky figure in chalk-white fringed war shirt and with a buffalo-horn bonnet on his aged head. His face was creased with years and exposure and his eyes were deep in his head, black, obsidian eyes, as level and impassive as the dark cliffs that lay behind them.

Kit spoke softly with a ringing sound. "White-Shield-Owner, Lige, sure as I'm a foot tall."

The Indian stopped a hundred feet away, leaned a little, then sat back again. He looked doubtful until Kit was closer, then he looked incredulous, disbelieving. "Ohiyesa," he said sharply in his native tongue. "Ohiyesa and Spitter."

"White-Shield-Owner."

The old chieftain stared for a long time, then he slid off his horse and squatted on the ground. Lige and Kit did the same. The coal-black eyes were thoughtful. "Are you the leader of these white people?"

"No," Kit said, "just their guide."

"They can't come any farther, Ohiyesa. This is sacred ground."

"They aren't going to stop, White-Shield-Owner. They are going as far as the setting sun."

"It doesn't matter," the old Indian said stubbornly. "They must turn back. Ohiyesa, I've had a hard time keeping the men of war back. You know me. I don't think what is happening will ever be settled with guns and arrows. You've heard me say this before. But I can't hold the young men much longer. Only until after we have spoken, Ohiyesa. After that, I can do nothing. Make them go back."

Kit crossed his legs under him. "White-Shield-Owner, you know me. I speak with a strong heart. I don't lie."

"*Owgh*," White-Shield-Owner grunted dourly. "You are our brother . . . but I can't stop the fighting men."

"Let the emigrants give you some horses, some whoa-haws, some powder and shot for your muzzleloaders, or some bullets for your soldier guns. Let them pay for crossing, but let them go by. They won't burn the grass or spoil the creeks."

White-Shield-Owner looked glumly, adamantly at Kit. "It cannot be, Ohiyesa. For two days now we have argued. For two days I have stood almost alone against them. They said I was too old to lead them, that I was a lover of whites, that the white men sent out the first soldiers, and now we will send out the second."

"There is no hope, White-Shield-Owner?"

"Hope? Yes. I can make the warriors leave them alone if they go back and don't wait too long. I can promise you that."

"Then," Kit said sadly, "my heart is on the ground." He watched the old Indian's face. White-Shield-Owner stared hard at him for a long moment before he spoke, then he smiled.

"We are brothers. My brother's bullet won't hurt as much as a stranger's. If we must fight, then it has been decided long ago that it must be so . . . but we are still brothers."

"We don't have to fight," Kit said.

The Dakota chieftain stood up. Kit and Lige got up, too. The Indian looked fondly at Kit. "It is written in our hearts, Ohiyesa," he said. "It has been decided. I have often thought that it might be this way between me and the white men I have hunted and raided and laughed with. Our paths are different, as our hides are."

Kit said nothing. In his mind was a pin prick of pain, as though he were seeing an old friend and a close one for the last time. There was no way he could make the Indian see his side of it and the emigrants had signified their determination. He struggled to show the same acceptance White-Shield-Owner showed. It was hard to do. He felt more sympathy for the Dakotas than he felt for the emigrants.

"You don't speak?"

"What can I say?"

White-Shield-Owner inclined his head once approvingly. "You are right. If we can't tell one another the truth without a forked tongue, then it is better to say nothing." He looked past Kit to the encircled wagons. His dark gaze was appraising and melancholy at the same time, as though there were two planes to his thoughts. "They can't be made to go back?"

"No."

There were lines gouged deep on each side of the Indian's prominent nose. His mouth showed bitterness but, strangely, his eyes held an odd gentleness. "*Dina sica*," he said softly, still looking at the thirty wagons drawn up for defense. "*Dina sica.*"

Kit repeated it, then said it in English. "No good . . . no good."

White-Shield-Owner turned and sprang onto his horse and held the single rein of his war bridle, looking down at the lean scout. "The men of war have a head for fighting only. It is so with both races. It is no good, Ohiyesa."

"Someday there will be peace," Kit said, raising his arm and pointing vaguely. "Over there."

White-Shield-Owner followed the symbol of the raised arm to the far, purpling distance. He understood and smiled dryly. "Yes, over there . . . someday. I am sorry." He turned and rode slowly back where the two warriors waited, his head low on his chest.

Kit rode back with Lige. He fought against the depth of melancholy that surged through him. It was useless; the grip of poignancy was too strong; the roots went too deep.

Lige was a profile, nothing else. A profile of hardship scored with experiences rarely pleasant. He was looking straight ahead, at the big circle with the animals and people inside, watching them ride back. "Damn," he said suddenly, fiercely, "I wish I'd never left the Indians."

When they got back, Powers and several other men came to see them. Kit faced them with his cloudy glance. "They won't let you pass. If you won't turn back, then you'll have to fight 'em."

"Couldn't you bribe the old devil?" a man asked.

Kit turned, saw the dark rush of rusty color under Lige's skin. He handed Lige his reins and motioned. Lige led the horses away with a fiery look but he said nothing.

Kit turned back and shook his head. "You can't bribe them. They do a thing for principle or they don't do it, but there's no way around what they make their minds up to."

Powers was looking steadily at Kit. "But we're outnumbered," he said in a protesting way.

"Then go back."

"We've come too far. Besides, if we went back, it wouldn't help. We'd run into them on another route."

It was true and Kit knew it was. The red man's domain was an invaded country. Every fighting buck, even the disabled, was rallying, spreading terror and devastation the length of their land. Fighting with every cruelty they knew and every brutality they could imagine, to throw back the white tide that was rolling onward, like locusts.

He turned away from the staring faces with a feeling of deep resentment for his own race. The dust was settling with its strong animal odors. He walked to an isolated part of the big circle where some horses drowsed unmindful of any danger, and until he stopped and gazed at the animals, enjoying their disregard of him, he wasn't conscious of the girl petting a black mare. She was looking straight at him.

"You're the scout, aren't you?"

He saw how black her hair was, like an Indian's. There were deep blue shadows in it. "I'm one of the scouts," he said, nodding.

"Those filthy red devils," she spat out violently.

It brought him up short. He looked back at her a second time. She was pretty. In fact, she was very pretty. Full-bodied with the cloth of her long dress drawn tightly over her flank and the shape of her face well-molded with large smoky eyes, a pert nose with a small saddle of freckles over its bridge, and a rich mouth over a jutting jaw, made that way now with the fierceness that was in her.

"They aren't filthy," he said with a little spirit.

Her eyes went through him. "Aren't they? They're like animals. You saw what they did this morning. You know what they do to captive women."

He began to shake his head in a harassed way as he always did when he met this same colossal ignorance of Indians. "Lady," he said with terrible patience, "they don't . . . do that . . . to white women. They make them slaves, kill them, or ransom them, but all that other . . . that's lies. White man lies. Sure, maybe some buck likes some one white woman, he might attack her, but Dakotas aren't at all like you've been told they are."

"You!" she said with a flood of anger. "You are defending them! They're filthy animals and that's all they are!"

"Not defending 'em, lady. I'm trying to explain them is all." He was rooted to the spot, watching the fury engulf her until her body almost shook. "There's never only one side to a fight . . . never."

"How about that boy this morning? What about the terrible tortures they inflict on people? What about their sickening pagan rites and their eating of raw meat and drinking warm blood?" She made a sound of deep repugnance.

"Lady, I just talked to an old Indian I've known for seven years. He said the whites sent out the first soldiers and the Indians sent out the second soldiers. That puts it pretty well, I think. This is their country, you know. They were here thousands of years before we were."

"This is America!"

"Well, I reckon it is. But only to us . . . not to the Indians. They say it is theirs. They've been here a long time."

"You agree with them?" Her gray glance was withering. He looked into it and squirmed inwardly from the scorn there, but he answered truthfully.

"Yes, in a lot of ways I do."

"You must be a good friend to them."

"I understand them, lady," he said. "When I see a bronco Indian, I kill him, if I can. That's the way it is out here. You kill him or he'll kill you."

"What chance did that boy have this morning?"

Kit frowned and returned her stare with one just as level and unfriendly, only in his gaze there was no open hostility such as she showed. "None. He didn't have a chance in the world. He might have thought he did when he rode out there, but he didn't. He was no more a match for an Indian in Indian country than any of the rest of these people."

"What had he ever done to a Sioux . . . tell me that."

"He probably hadn't even seen a Sioux before," Kit said, "but other whites have. They've shot them on sight for the past ten years. That's all that matters to the Sioux. The whites are all against them. Then they are all against the whites!"

"You make it sound like civilized warfare."

He grinned at that. "I didn't know there was

such a thing," he said dryly. "Any warfare I've ever seen hasn't been what I'd call civilized. Lady, no one knows who fired the first shot now. All we know is that it was fired. Does that make sense to you?"

"But we can't treat them like human beings. They aren't."

His irritation returned swiftly. "I don't see how you can say that. You've never sat down with them, listened to them talk, seen them laugh and play pranks on one another."

"They're heathens!"

Kit shook his head at her. "No, they have a god . . . I'm not sure he isn't the same God we're supposed to believe in, either."

She lapsed into silence, looking at him. The black mare was drowsing in the late afternoon sun with her eyes half closed and her head hanging. He thought it made a picture like that. The nice mare and the girl's arm thrown across her withers, the smoke-gray of her eyes and the fullness of her body, the slight, fading frown on her forehead and the little defiant droop to the outer corners of her full lips.

"Will they let us go on?"

He shook his head. "No."

Her eyes clouded over again swiftly. "Then . . . what?"

"Why, I reckon we either go back or fight past them."

She regarded his stoical calmness with a puzzled look.

"You aren't worried?"

"Worried? Sure I'm worried, but I'm here and alone. I can't begin to ride all the way back. Alone I can't go ahead, either."

"You said you were their friend."

"I am," he said, then he stopped. "It's too long a story. You wouldn't understand anyway."

"Tell me," she said quickly. Then slower: "I've never met a white man like you . . . who talked *for* them."

"I'm their friend so long as we look at things the same way . . . like with white people. Now I'm against them . . . well, not exactly, but at least I'm against their stopping the wagons or turning them back. So . . . I'll fight them."

"Do they know you? I mean, do they know who you are and that you are guiding us?" He inclined his head. "What did they say to that?" she asked.

Kit smiled a little at her. "The one I talked to said it wouldn't hurt as much to be shot by a brother as it would to be shot by a stranger."

She took her arm from the black mare's neck and gripped her hands together, locking the fingers tightly. "I am afraid," she said softly.

"So am I," Kit said.

"You don't look it," she said with spirit, almost spitefully.

He laughed. "Well, I am just the same. Maybe in a different way than you are."

She looked past him at the raw sweep of the land. "I hate this," she said, moving her head to indicate the country. "It's primitive, cruel and primitive."

He looked away from her and studied the country with its outfall of long, slender shadows. Its huge sweeps of blood red sunlight dying in a splashed and awesome way across the immense mountains, and the waving grass, fat with nourishment for horses and game. "No, it isn't the country. The country's beautiful. Every mile of it. It's the fear that's got you, lady, not the land."

He left her after that, feeling better for some strange reason, and walked down to where Lige had a tiny fire going. He dropped down with a sigh and a grunt and wagged his head at the older man. "Where'd the Dakotas go?"

Lige tossed his head. "Back into the damned trees," he said, "where they can get a little rest before they hit us about dawn." As though dismissing the grimness, Lige fished around with one hand on his off-side and brought up two soggy-looking lumps of dough. "Look here, real white man's bread. I talked a woman out of it. She was beating up a batch in a big crock." Lige eyed the lumpy mass with infinite tenderness. "We'll bake it in the coals after we eat. Be just right for breakfast."

Kit was pointing. "Look, Lige."

A black, oily spiral of smoke was rising straight up in the hushed, sparkling stillness. Lige looked and put the dough back on the ground with a slow movement. "Indian signals. Well, those aren't the only ones around, then. Hell of a skittle now, for sure. Outnumbered before . . . what'll we be by dawn?"

"Maybe it's just a try at getting reinforcements. If they had friends close, they wouldn't bother with a thing like that. They'd send a messenger for 'em."

Lige studied the smoke for a long time, in between his cooking chores. "One thing, Kit. If they don't get any help by morning, fine. If they do, that yellow hair of yours'll look real pert atop a coup stick."

Chapter Four

They ate and Kit sat hunched over, looking into the coals when Lige made the little cavities in the earth where he put the bread dough to bake. Powers came over after full nightfall and dropped down. Lige looked around at him and squinted. "Did you put out double guards?" he asked.

Powers bobbed his head. "One ring 'way out. Another closer in and a scattering of men just beyond the wagons."

"Stagger 'em?" Kit asked.

"Yes. If they come tonight, they'll get a hot welcome."

"They won't come in force," Kit said, "but I reckon a few glory hunters'll try to lift a little hair on their own."

Powers mused. He had taken every precaution. There was fear in him but it was neither the same kind the girl had felt nor the kind that was lying like a small steel ball in Kit's stomach. With Powers it was dread. "You fellers think there's any way out besides fighting?"

Lige went on worrying over the coals where his bread dough lay. He said nothing with his customary way of making his silence shout. Kit watched the silhouettes that were people. It made him wince the way they would let themselves be illuminated by the little cooking fires. “No way other than what you’ve decided, and they’ve decided.”

“But we *can’t* go back!” Powers burst out passionately. Then he checked himself.

“So,” Kit said smoothly, “I reckon you’d better go up forward and get what sleep you can. And say, Powers . . . when you go past those folks up there, you might tell them to stay to hell away from their fires. If a buck gets through the guards, he could pot-shoot a half dozen of the fools.”

Powers was getting up when another figure came out of the night, close by. All three men looked up, startled. Only Kit recognized her. Lige was spellbound, his jaw hung. Five weeks—nearly six—and he had never seen her before.

“Mister Powers,” she said, glancing swiftly away from Kit.

“Why, Allie.” Powers got the rest of the way to his feet with an effort. He smiled at her and looked down at the scouts. “Boys, this is Miss Allison Burgess. Folks call her Allie.”

“Proud, ma’am,” Lige found the wits to say, closing his mouth with a noise afterward as if it were a steel trap.

Kit smiled sardonically and said nothing until Powers peered at him, then he nodded. “We’ve met before.” He motioned toward a saddle blanket where Lige had been sitting. “Sit down, Miss Burgess.”

She sank down, and Lige moved sideways to see her better, his eyes like chips of ice. Powers seemed uncertain whether to stay or leave. Kit looked steadily at him. He left.

"I . . . I wanted to hear more about these Indians, Mister Butler."

"Kit. My name's Christopher. They call me Kit." He nodded toward Lige. "My pardner could tell you more than I can. He's lived with just about every tribe in the Northwest."

Allie Burgess looked at Lige and the old mountain man froze for a moment before he smiled at her. Beauty was a thing a man might go ten years without seeing in the far country. White beauty, anyway. Lige shrugged uncomfortably. "Kit's better at telling it. He knows as much as I do anyway, ma'am."

But Kit wasn't ready to expound. He watched her face, the way the dying light highlighted it. She was beautiful—not pretty, after all, but beautiful. The black hair shone with an imprisoned luster. "Ma'am, how come your folks are migrating?"

"Why? We're against slavery, that's why."

Kit's smile was slight and rueful, like his words. "You can't ever lick anything by running from it."

"We're not running."

Lige heard the deepening sharpness of her voice and looked quickly at Kit.

"If you aren't, what're you doing 'way out here in Dakota country?"

"My father wants to find a country where the land is good and there's no slavery. We've heard about California. Have you ever been there, Mister Butler?"

"Kit," he said again gravely. "No ma'am, and unless I'm wrong, half the United States'll be out there in another few years. I don't want to get that far into the desert."

"It's no desert," she said quickly.

"Like Indians are filthy heathens. The same way. You've never seen Indians and you've never seen California, but one's no good and the other's heaven on earth."

She had the smoky look in her eyes. He couldn't see it but he knew it was there by the expression of both hardness and antagonistic defiance that swept over her face. She said nothing. He remembered the way she did that, too. Let silence create awkwardness. He looked at the fire and stiffened with a quick grunt.

"The bread, Lige. Consarn it, the bread!"

Lige strangled a curse and dug frantically. The smells arose before Lige had more than gotten the first layer of earth off. "Burned," he groaned. "Burned to a frazzle, Kit." The look of abjection made Kit grin, then smile, then laugh out loud at the expression Lige wore.

Allie Burgess caught the drift of their dilemma and laughed, too. The sound was deep and husky and soft, like the earth cooling after a drenching rain in midsummer, warm and refreshing.

Lige swung and gazed at her. "It's funny to you, ma'am," he said. "But that there's the first real honest-to-God, woman-made bread dough we've had in years."

She looked fixedly at Lige. "It can't be," she said.

"Well, it is, lady," Lige said stubbornly. "We've been eating *wasna* ration and greens and buffalo hump for longer'n I'd care to guess at." He swung toward Kit with an injured air. "Isn't that gospel truth, Kit?"

"Yes, ma'am. Indians don't make bread. Especially Dakota Indians. They live on meat almost entirely. Buffalo hump, mule meat, horse meat, antelope, elk, deer . . . just about anything, including dog . . . but not much else."

"No vegetables? No bread of any kind? Not even that corn cake-looking bread the Mexicans had back at Independence?"

"Yes, ma'am. In the spring and summer the Indians get wild onions and the like, but no bread. Not even the Mexican stuff."

She held his glance a long time. "Well, I'll get you some bread." She hesitated, frowning a little. "Didn't any of the other pioneers give you any?"

Kit's smile returned sardonically. He shook his head. "We're not invited to supper, ma'am. You saw how they'd've eaten us alive today, I expect. No, we're like Indians to you folks. Guides and scouts as far as Fort Collins . . . after that a dirty memory of a harrowing passage over hostile Indian country."

"You're exaggerating," she said sharply, getting up. "I'll go get you some fresh bread."

She was turning away when Kit stopped her. "No. You just go back to your wagon and stay there. Take a gun and stay low and out of sight, and Miss Allie . . . don't walk in front of any of those cussed little cooking fires on the way back."

He watched her go. Lige sat with his hands dangling, looking after her. He swore gently. "Kit, I never saw her before."

"I didn't, either, until this afternoon. Well, like I told her, we don't mix much."

"She's as pretty a filly as I've seen in years. In fact," Lige said flatly, "I'm not so sure she's not the prettiest woman I've *ever* saw."

Kit tossed a pebble into the fire. He didn't speak, and after a while Lige looked back at the two lumps of blackened bread batter. "Who's going to sleep first?"

"You can," Kit said. "I've run into too many ghosts today to be able to sleep . . . for a while anyway."

"What do you mean?"

"Oh, White-Shield-Owner for one. That red-headed fellow losing his hair for another. I've seen that done before, on a dead run. It sort of sticks inside your mind, Lige."

"And the girl, Kit?"

"Roll in and shut up. I'm going for a walk. I'll take a look at their guard. I'll wake you in a few hours."

Lige watched his lean, tall form move away. He felt around for his old buffalo robe, rolled up into it, and lay there looking up at the lanterns in the sky.

Kit leaped over a wagon tongue that ran half the distance of the wagon in front of it. Outside the wagon circle the night seemed less friendly, less inhabited and intimate, more foreign, more Indian. He shrugged away the thoughts that came flooding. It was eerie, though, waiting, waiting, knowing what was coming at dawn, and being reasonably safe right now, even with the knowledge that a dozen black eyes were watching the emigrant train.

He saw the first man off on his right, about fifty feet ahead. He spoke before he moved any closer. The man swung with his rifle, making a vicious half circle.

"That you, Samuel?"

No. Kit Butler, the scout." He went forward until he could see the man's face. It was a dark night. Only the slimmest of moons shone weakly. He recognized the man suddenly. It was the man Powers had called Reaves, the man who had been hot-eyed and fiery-faced after the killing of the youth in the morning. He nodded stiffly at him. "Seen anything?"

"Nary a thing. Man sure can think he sees 'em, though. And hears 'em. While ago I'd a-swore they was in the grass. They wasn't." Reaves smelled strongly of chewing tobacco, a bitter-sweet smell.

Kit studied the stillness with its purple reflection. There wasn't a sound ahead, or a movement, and yet there could be. . . . "Pretty night," he said suddenly, looking upward. The man called Reaves shot him a startled glance. He said nothing. Kit's glance dropped. "Where's the rest of them? Up ahead a ways?"

"Yeah. Caleb Martin's to the right of us. Watch him, though. Old Cal's touchy tonight." The man's face swung swiftly, close to Kit's face. His voice was husky and hoarse and very low. "Will they hit us at dawn, Butler? What d'you think?"

"I think they'll come," Kit said, moving away. "We'll know in a few hours."

He walked away from Reaves in a southerly direction. He didn't want to see any more of the guards. It was the restless desire to be alone that had driven him out here in the first place.

The night was an immense vault. He sat down on the ground and felt the night dampness of the grass. *Will they hit us at dawn, Butler?* He swore, something he rarely ever did. Hit us? They'll come like a whirlwind, raising the yell. They'll make the ground rumble with the drum roll of their horses. They'll come all right. Like the most diabolical devils any stay-at-home has ever imagined when he was re-telling the horrors other stay-at-homes had written or imagined or just plain made up.

He smiled at the night and lived within himself, recalling raids he had made with friendly Indians against their enemies. He thought of White-Shield-Owner and marveled that the old man of war had thought so far ahead as to see, long ago, that he and Kit might be enemies. He had thought about it enough to think it through.

My brother's bullet won't hurt as much as a stranger's. . . .

He looked at the faint outline, bold and yet soft, of the far-away hills and somewhere deep within him there arose an urge to pray as the Indians prayed. He bent his head and chanted an old Arapaho prayer.

Father, have pity on me.
Father, have pity on them.
I am crying for thirst.
They are crying for thirst.
All is gone . . . my soul is empty.
Their souls are empty,
Have mercy on them.

He looked up into the night again and thought of the girl. He could picture the look of shock and abhorrence on her face if she had heard him chanting an Indian prayer. He laughed under his breath and even formed the words with his lips. *It is the same God. If they believe in one Great Spirit and you believe in the same Great Spirit under another name, Allie Burgess . . . who can say He isn't the same God?*

Like a slow awakening, then, he understood what his restlessness was. The girl. Not the Dakotas—the girl with the Indian-black hair with blue shadows in it, the smoky gray eyes, the full-lipped mouth, and the hatred for Indians.

With realization came a manner of peace. He gazed steadily ahead. The hours fled by, and only when he saw the faint grayness did his heart slam hard against his ribs. He jumped up and turned back, hurrying. Any time now. . . .

The wagon circle was still and quiet. He had a panicky thought that the emigrants might be asleep, after all. He shook it off and trotted back with the dew making his boots shine with dampness. He saw the guard, Reaves, and called to him.

"Watch close now, pardner. If they're coming, it won't be long."

The guard hardly moved. His face was sagging and gray-looking. Kit stopped when he was almost back to the wagons and twisted for a long glance backward. The land was ill-looking, quiet with a hush of death, and murky-looking. Against the far forest there was a starkness of limbs and trunks and ghostliness, a deep-brooding expectancy. He turned and went almost to the wagon tongue. In fact, he was reaching for it with his hand when he heard what might have passed the other hearers as a soft, distant soughing of wind in the long grass. A long, piercing cry rendered soft and mellow with distance.

"*Hoka Hay*!"

He cleared the barrier in a swift leap, drew his pistol, and fired it once into the air, then he ran toward Lige Turner and wrenched away the buffalo robe. Lige sat up heavily, gropingly, fighting for clearness. He saw the tight face above him and came to his feet with his carbine in his hand. He blinked away the surplus water in his eyes.

"Are they coming, Kit?"

"Listen!"

The wagon train was bursting with life now and the guards had seen and were rushing back with their mouths open and no sounds coming out. They all heard it the second time, but only two of the nearly two hundred understood it.

"*Hoka Hay*!" It meant: "Charge!"

"God Almighty," Lige said fluidly. "Come on!"

Chapter Five

The wagon circle was a throng of confusion. Men's rumbling shouts rose when there was no need for them beyond the primordial desire to yell and so dissipate pent-up tension that had been growing under their hearts for days.

The contagion spread to the horses and cattle. People had to hug close to the big wagons, for frightened horses careened by wildly. Kit watched, with a helpless feeling, how the emigrants reacted to the final test. Only the younger men seemed to go directly to the places where their gunfire would help. He thought instinctively that this was a land that consumed youth, ate it up, and wore it out fighting, building, toiling over the terrible deserts and mountains and flooding rivers, then tossed it aside and reached for new youth to consume. He turned and sought Lige. The mountain man was already rolling a thick oaken water cask with grunting effort.

Together they worried the cask under a wagon and lay down behind it. Lige's jaws were locked so that his cheeks looked ribbed with muscle. Kit wormed around the cover a little and lay with his head low, peering out. The bedlam behind, and around them, was deafening.

He saw the Dakotas coming in a flung-out

charge. The closer they got the more their spine-tingling screams overrode the noise within the wagon circle. It wasn't a case of any one warrior leading them. The warrior who got close first was simply the warrior who rode the fastest horse. None of them seemed occupied with their single rein, but all had the loosely looped catch rope tucked under their belts. This catch rope was often as long as forty feet and it trailed on their right side. Its sole purpose was to enable an unhorsed warrior to retain his horse before the fleeing animal got away.

"They didn't get any reinforcements!" Lige shouted to him. "No more now'n there was yesterday!"

Kit nodded but made no attempt to shout back. The war cries drowned out all sound now. There was a quick rataplan of gunfire from within the circle. Kit swung, frowning, and peered out at the emigrants. They were everywhere. Prone, under wagons as he and Lige were, standing recklessly in plain sight over wagon tongues, and moving through the thick, heavy dust stirred up by the panicked animals. The Indians were far out of range yet, but the emigrants were trying for looping shots. Kit made a disgusted face and swung back to watch the Indians sweep into range.

He expected them to split off and enfilade the circle. They didn't. They came on in their ragged, unorganized charge, low over their horses' necks, and swept by on the far south side of the wagons. The gunfire was like a dirge. It made his ears ring.

The vivid kaleidoscope was engulfed in a great curling cloud of dun dust from within and without the circle. Kit squinted hard to see if they would swing inward and try to breach the wagon circle. He couldn't even see the southern-most wagons and the furor of sound made a guess impossible.

The Dakotas swept by, their eerie cries ringing above the crash of erratic, rapid gunfire. Kit watched the mass of dust-laden men moving as they followed the riding attackers in their frenzy to get in final shots.

Lige started squirming out from under the wagon. Kit grabbed his shirt and yelled: "Lie low! Wait! They'll be back!"

They came back, too, only in a large arc that brought them up the far north side of the circle. Lige was swearing and crawling around the water cask for a shot when Kit saw their first target. The buck was swinging down on the off-side of his racing animal when Kit fired. Lige, from much experience, waited.

The horse went end over end, throwing the warrior like a pinwheel. The Indian grabbed frantically for his catch rope. He had it in both hands and was lurching to his feet when Lige's big-bore gun exploded. The buck jumped high into the air and fell in a lifeless sprawl. The howling Dakotas streamed past, kicking up another dust cloud.

"One!" Lige shouted, reloading.

The earth shook and the noise was deafening. Gunshots smashed through the dust and a powerful smell of horse sweat and gunpowder filtered through the racket and haziness. Behind them, emigrants were running across the circle, yelling.

Kit saw the big bay horse with balled ears, belly down, in a frantic race. The warrior on his back was swinging a carbine with his body, tracking something with his sights. Kit aimed and the two guns went off almost in concert. The buck flinched and was lost in the dust. Kit swore, rolled, and looked back. Two emigrants were standing stunned, unbelieving, staring down at a third man.

Lige's stubby carbine with its cavernous mouth bellowed a mighty blast. It was the final shot.

As suddenly as the action had begun, it stopped. One of those dreadful, impromptu silences that descend freakishly in battles came down with startling clarity. Everyone froze as though turned to stone, held immobile and startled for just a second, then the shouts and cries went up again.

By that time the Indians were far down the valley out of range.

"Two, to your one and near hit," Lige said warmly, as if he was at a turkey shoot.

Kit rolled over and rested his head against the

cask, watching the embattled emigrants. “Pioneers,” he said contemptuously. “They call themselves pioneers. Hell, did you see how they ran across that open ground?”

“Yeah. Bet half of ’em stood right between the wagons and let the danged Indians shoot at ’em.”

“They’ve got a lot to learn,” Kit said, working his way from under the wagon.

“Powers’ll teach ’em,” Lige said sourly, following Kit out. He stretched and watched the white men carting off the body of the man who had fallen near them.

Kit said nothing. Until that moment the possibility of fire arrows hadn’t crossed his mind. Now they did. “Funny, Lige. No fires.”

“Oh, hell,” the older man said dryly, “that was just the hot-bloods getting their dander worked out. They’ll be back.”

Kit saw Allie Burgess once, just a glimpse of her tall silhouette through the settling haze of the yellow dust. He started around the wagon circle toward her. Lige watched his course, hesitated, shrugged, and squatted by their fire hole, which had been badly mauled by men and horses. He felt around for his twist of Kentucky chewing tobacco.

Kit saw that Allie Burgess’s hands had blood on them and that her face was like chalk. Something in the back of his mind warned him against approaching her now, but he went up anyway, where she was kneeling beside a wounded man with a gory, shattered arm.

"Glad you're all right, ma'am."

She shot him a worried, hectic look. "I'm fine . . . no thanks to your Indians."

The warning came back twice as strong. He stood hip-shot, watching the sure way she worked, feeling awkward and a mite embarrassed that he was all in one piece when so many of the emigrants weren't. "What're the casualties, do you know?"

"No one knows yet, Mister Butler. It's too soon. So far I've worked on seven wounded myself, and the other women are busy, too."

He was appalled. One flashing attack by exuberant men of war who weren't more than showing off, really, and the emigrants had been whittled down badly. He kneeled and watched her working with the man's arm, unseeingly.

The worst was yet to come. He wasn't conscious of her steady, hard glance at all. He was worried. Getting up swiftly, he went in search of Powers, the wagon boss. When he found him, his surprise was even greater. Powers was dead!

"Anyone see it happen?"

"Yes," an old man with a powder-burned face said with a slow nod. "I was right beside him. They come a-whoopin' and he let off just one shot. That was afore they was 'thin range . . . and plunk! Right through the brisket."

"Arrow?" Kit asked, looking down at the old gaffer.

"Nope, gunshot."

"Where were you two standing?"

The old fellow turned and pointed at a space where a wagon tongue separated the front of one big Conestoga from the rear of another wagon. "There," he said. "Me, I was under the danged thing. Powers was standin'. . . ."

"Yeah. Thanks." Kit's anger worked slowly. It wasn't until he was back where Lige was laboriously blowing on a new little cooking fire that it was fully matured. It showed in the smoldering sheen of his eyes. Lige looked up at him, bent to blow on the fire again, then raised his head for a second, longer look.

"What's stung you, Kit?"

"Powers is dead."

Lige nodded thoughtfully, then bent and blew on the fire for a moment before he spoke. "No hell of a loss," he said. "I never cared for him. Big hero one minute, danged cry baby the next."

"I'm not thinking of Powers. They've got about thirty hurt."

"Couldn't have," Lige said with a quickening frown. "Why, hell, boy . . ."

"They have, Lige."

Lige sank back on his haunches, looking at Kit. It was inconceivable to him. The emigrants had had cover. The Dakotas were riding fast, making accurate aim nearly impossible. "Thirty!" He made a snorting sound through his nose. "Now what?"

"I don't know, but if they don't start using their heads for something beside Indian targets, there won't be enough left to drive their cussed wagons to Fort Collins."

The camp became a place of abiding gloom and sadness. Even the uninjured went listlessly about the business of burying the dead and caring for the wounded. The lugubrious atmosphere didn't bother Lige. He fried two steaks of antelope haunch and hunted Kit up to give him one. The sobs rolled off Lige like water off a rock. He ate and watched and said nothing.

Kit found two emigrants engaged in a nervous argument over a successor to Powers. He walked up to them with his antelope steak, and listened for a moment, then he turned swiftly away with disgust on his face.

Allie Burgess found him watching the people, leaning beside her parents' wagon, chewing slowly. He looked philosophically calm and placid. It aroused her ire when he glanced up, met her stare, and nodded gently.

"I don't see anything to be so calm about, Mister Butler."

"Kit," he said, looking past her where four graves were being hastily covered. "I'm not calm."

"You look it."

"Maybe. I'm more scairt than you are, now."

"There's a little consolation in that," she said waspishly.

"More scairt," he repeated, watching the flinty chunks of soil go into the graves from spades in the hands of white-faced men who sweated copiously. "Because if these people were hurt this bad when there was no call for it, what'll happen to them when they *really* have to fight?"

"What was this," she said fiercely, her smoky eyes like wet slate, "if it wasn't a battle?"

"This wasn't *the* battle, ma'am. The battle's yet to come."

"What do you mean?" A little fear was coming in where the fury had been. "Why wasn't this *the* battle?"

"Well, they work like this. First, the wise men let the hot-bloods . . . the men of war . . . have a fling. That's what we just skirmished through. Now, after some of the hot-bloods have been killed and we're still down here, why the old men get together and have their licks. They use strategy, not head-on tactics like the coup hunters use."

She tried to catch his glance and couldn't. He was watching the graves fill with an unblinking, unseeing dourness. "Will they try it again, today?"

He looked at her then. "Yes, maybe in an hour or so."

"They can't," she said desperately, squirting the words out.

"Because we're not ready?" he asked softly. "Why, ma'am, I don't reckon that'll keep 'em back very long."

"Oh," she said. "Oh."

He saw how tired she looked and it made an uneasy stirring inside of him in his chest. He threw aside the last of the steak, wiped his fingers very methodically on his trousers, and gazed at her in silence.

"They've killed the wagon boss," she said.

"I know. Leaders aren't important out here, Allie, unless they know how to do things . . . and when."

She wanted to say something, just anything that would jar his appearance of complacency. It seemed an impossible thing to do. He was leaning there in the shade as calm-looking, as collected and thoughtful as though he were a thousand miles away back in Independence.

Then he spoke in the same soft, gentle way, looking at her. "They got a lot of tricks. Folks'll tell you they ride around and around a wagon circle. Well, that's not true. They make one hot-blood attack like that, then, if that doesn't work, they fall back on strategy. Just like white soldiers do."

"There's no comparison," she shot at him sharply.

He shrugged, let his gaze fall away from her face, and in that moment saw the emigrants wandering aimlessly, listlessly through the dust and over the trampled, soft-churned earth, and an idea was born. He got a quick, tense look. She saw it come, a speculative coldness mixed with deep resentment.

"You don't like these people, do you?"

"It isn't that," he said candidly and swiftly, his mantle of seeming indifference gone suddenly. "I'm with them now and can't help myself, that's all. They're fools. They call themselves pioneers. They're emigrants . . . that's what we call 'em out here and that's what they are. Emigrants. Learners. It's the same thing. Look at them. Instead of getting ready, they're wandering around like gut-shot buffalo. Look at them."

His scorn stung her anew. "How do you expect them to act differently without leadership?" she demanded hotly.

His eyes went back to her face. She was more alluring now, dust, grime, anger and all, than he had ever seen her look. "For God's sake, Allie. There's still a hundred and fifty of them. Powers wasn't the only man here."

"All right," she said ringingly, her voice mounting with passion. "Why don't you lead them?"

"Me?"

"Yes, you! Since *you* know what the redskins're going to do and *they* don't . . . and your life's as much at stake as mine and theirs . . . why don't you help yourself and them, too?"

He was too engrossed with the idea to answer. She misunderstood his silence. Her eyes grew smoky. She let the staring moment of vibrant silence settle. He saw how she did it; it thrilled something deep within him and he smiled at her. "All right, Allie. All right. I'll do it. I'll try it, anyway, and if they don't want to listen, you won't blame me?"

"Of course not, Mister Butler." Her voice was tight and a little harsh. "Why should I, if you offer them your services?"

He reached for the iron tire of a high rear wheel, twisted to face it, to spring up where they could all see and hear him, then he paused a moment and looked back at her. "In case I never get the chance to tell you this again, ma'am. I think you're the most beautiful woman I've ever seen."

Then he sprang up, balanced on the huge wheel, and let out a Dakota scream. It was effective enough. The emigrants froze where they were, looking wildly at him. "Listen to me, folks," he said in a deep, throbbing voice. "You've lost a leader. Maybe you can elect one after this is over, but right now I want you to do what I tell you."

He saw their faces, intent and dirty with sweat. Men straightened up and stared.

"Those Indians'll be back shortly. You haven't won a fight. Hell, you haven't even *begun* to fight

’em. Now then . . . you, there . . . you with the beaver hat. Take ten men and draw off buckets of water. Put ’em under the seat of every wagon. That’s in case they use fire arrows when they come back.” The people were looking interested now. The men moved in a little, a lot of the thralldom faded from their faces. A few even smiled and showed in the shine of their eyes they liked what they heard.

“And, Reaves . . . you pick ten more men and haul stuff out of those cussed wagons and build barricades under them.” He saw Lige stroll up with a surprised look on his face. He smiled down at him. “Lige, count their ball and powder and bullets. See that everyone’s got the same amount. Let me know how we stand that way. Show ’em how to make a barricade, Lige, and the first grown man who stands between the wagons, kick him in the britches as hard as you can.”

Lige swallowed and flushed. His eyes twinkled sardonically. “You reckon to make prairie warriors out of sheep, Kit?” he called out.

Someone laughed. Kit smiled. The people had their hope renewed. There was a surging glow inside Kit. He started to climb down from the wheel, hesitated, and let his grin slide off sideways. “Listen, folks. I don’t have any notion how long they’ll keep us bottled up here. Maybe two days, maybe a week, but I *do* know what’ll happen if you ever let them inside this circle. It isn't a pretty thing to talk about, but if some of you want to know privately, come around and I'll tell you. Above everything else . . . don't expose yourself . . . don't sleep or drowse under the wagons . . . and *don't let an Indian inside this circle!*"

He leaped down and stood beside Allie Burgess. She was watching his profile. His eyes danced and his face was a rust color from the swift-running blood under it.

"You were very good," she said softly. "I'm glad."

He looked at her searchingly. "Glad I'm good?"

"No, glad you did that. They believe in you, Mister Bu . . ."

"Kit."

"They do. Look at them." She was avoiding his glance and he knew it. He smiled a little dourly and watched the emigrant women resist the stony-faced egress of the men who tossed out marble-topped bureau, parts of mahogany bedsteads, and even barrels of salt pork and flour. Over it all he heard Lige's stuttering protest to the women, that salted flour made the best bullet and arrow stopper there was.

"Will they come after dark?"

He had forgotten her standing there. He shook his head, watching. "No. I already told you they don't fight at night. Listen, Allie, this was your idea. Why don't you go help Lige? Look at those women. You'd think a barrel of flour or salt pork was more valuable to them than their husbands' lives."

"All right," she said.

He watched her cross the enclosure. It was going to be a fight for survival. He knew it, and after a little while the emigrants would find it out, know it, too. Survival called forth every effort. He went among the men, picking one out here and there, until he had assembled thirty riflemen. He led them up where the animals were nuzzling for food and motioned for them to sit on the ground.

"Now listen, boys. You know this is going to be a fight, but you don't know how much of a fight it's going to be, and I'm here to tell you right now that if any of us ride out of this valley, it'll only be because of you men. I want you to do exactly what I tell you the second I say it. You understand?"

The men nodded. They looked almost eager. The bustle and excitement within the circle lent them an eagerness they hadn't had before.

"All right. The first thing is this. You follow me. Wherever I go, dammit, you follow. No questions, no hanging back. Just follow. The second thing is this . . . don't . . . I don't care a damn what you think privately . . . but don't fire a shot until I tell you to. Agreed?"

The men spoke clearly in agreement when a tousled youth with ice-chip eyes of very clear blue spoke up. "Will they be back?"

"Be back?" Kit said. "They'll be back before you know it, and this time you'll think they're going on by like they did before . . . only they won't. This time, if you fight like you did last time, they'll breach the circle. After that, that hair of yours'll hang from a war bridle like a curb strap, or from a lance or coup stick. This time will tell the tale . . . but even after they come this second time, the fight'll be one hell of a long way from over. Now go over where Lige is and check your guns and ammunition with him."

The men stepped out briskly. Kit stayed back and watched them. He tingled pleasantly with a feeling he had never known before.

"Here's something for you . . . General."

"Allie?"

She was holding out something wrapped in a piece of clean white cloth. He took it and laid back the cloth. "A loaf of white bread. White-flour bread. Well, I'll be . . ."

"Please." She winced. "You really do swear too much."

"Me? Why, I hardly ever swear."

"Every time I've been around you, it seemed to me you swore."

"Well, like I told you, I'm scairt. Anyway, if you think I swear, you ought to hear Lige."

"I know," she said quickly, color high under each eye. "I just gave him a loaf and walked away."

He tore the loaf in two, smelled it, and started to eat.

The tingling sensation became a depth of satisfaction so strong and overwhelming he sighed and squatted. She looked down at him with a hint of amusement. "Can't you just lean on something like most white men? Do you always have to squat or sit on the ground like an Indian?"

"Excuse me." He got up, blushing, walked to the nearest wagon, and leaned on it. She had washed her face and swept back the ebony wealth of her hair in a severe, parted way. A small red ribbon held the long residue. It fell like a midnight cascade down her back. The bread almost choked him the way his throat tightened up. "Allie? You wouldn't like it if an Indian lover talked sweet to you, would you?"

"No," she said bluntly, giving him stare for stare until his look fell away, crestfallen.

"Well . . . thought I'd ask," he mumbled.

"Everyone else is working, Mister . . ."

"Kit."

"Why don't you and I?"

"Did you talk to the womenfolk?"

"Yes."

"Well, you could make things ready for the wounded. Get lard and goose grease and poultices and such-like ready."

"I did that right after the skirmish."

"Oh." He ate more bread, at a loss.

She swung swiftly toward him and smiled. It was like the sun coming after a gray rain. "Maybe," she said very fast, so that each word followed on the tail of the former word. "Maybe after this is all over." Then she walked swiftly back up toward the place where emigrant women were pooling resources and rolling bandages.

He stood frowning, chewing slowly and thoughtfully. *Maybe what?* It didn't make sense.

Lige came over with a harassed look. He was clutching his half-eaten bread in a grimy paw. "They got enough shot to last three, four days, even the way *they* shoot. I give 'em hell about that over-shooting." He turned and squatted beside Kit on the ground and looked up where the men were making barricades. "Funny thing, ain't it? I never thought they had it in 'em, Kit."

"I reckon anyone'll fight like a grizzly when they've got to, Lige."

"No, I didn't mean that. I meant I didn't know they'd ever get the hang of *how* to fight Indians."

Kit gulped the last of his bread and swept away the crumbs with a brisk gesture. "They haven't fought 'em yet. They look like they'll make out all right, but you can't ever tell. Not right up until White-Shield-Owner's bucks come straight at them. If they break, we're done for."

Lige ate placidly, grunting around a mouthful. "*Owgh*. It'll scare the tarnation out of 'em when they see that. Did you warn 'em about a charge?"

"No. What for? They'll see one soon enough. Why scare 'em ahead of time? Anyway, I've picked thirty or so of the hardest-looking bucks among them. I'm betting on them to turn back a big charge, Lige."

"Where do you want me?"

"Sort of go among 'em, Lige. Keep them from showing themselves. I think when they get excited they'll be a little careless about that. Move among 'em and keep 'em fighting. Watch they don't get drawn out of the circle, too."

Kit moved away, stopped a few feet off, turned and frowned at Lige. "Why don't you lean on things, Lige, like a white man does," he said, "instead of always squatting like a cussed Indian?" Then he went to the nearest wagon tongue, vaulted over it, and strode swiftly across the grass beyond.

Lige got up like he'd been sitting on a snake. He turned in a bewildered way and regarded the ground, then glanced over where Kit had disappeared and frowned. Blood rushed angrily into his face. "Well, I'll be double-damned," he said indignantly.

Chapter Six

Beyond the wagons there was a smear of dead Indian horses here and there. Of dead warriors, Kit counted four. It made him shake his head. Easily a hundred rounds fired and four dead hostiles. He felt like swearing, but didn't.

A long way off there was the telltale dust to show where the Indians were. He walked out boldly for a half a mile before he saw three mounted Indians, sentinels, watching the wagon train. He studied them carefully, keeping track of the distance back, then he squatted and narrowed his eyes against the distance, trying to guess what the Dakotas were doing.

Men were walking horses, leading them up and down, limbering their best war horses. He grunted to himself. There would be another attack before long.

The dazzling sunlight shone off metal, far up the valley. He studied the sun. It was hardly noon. He got up and started back with his long, springing stride. There would be another attack today.

The circle looked strong from where he was. He took especial notice of the undersides of the big Conestogas. There wasn't much daylight visible. He kept an eye on the Dakota sentinels but they seemed disinclined to try and get close enough to fight him.

Back inside the circle he hunted up his hand-picked riflemen and took them to the west side of the circle, rousted out the men who were already there, and sent his own men under in their places. "Remember what I told you now. Don't shoot, no matter what, until I give you the order."

"Where'll you be?" a man asked.

"Don't worry about me. When I want you to fire, I'll let you know."

Lige came over with a disagreeable look. "Say, Kit, about that squatting on the . . ."

"Kit!"

He spun without seeking the man who had called him. Lige ran briskly beside him. They went to the nearest gap between wagons and looked for what a sentinel had seen.

The Indians were coming back, only they were trotting, not running their horses. "Talk," Lige said. "Council." Kit nodded in silence, watching. Someone fired a gun. With a sizzling oath Lige turned wrathfully and went hurrying up the line to find the man. It was silent after that, so silent Kit heard someone walking up behind him. Irritably he turned. It was Allie Burgess.

"I'm sorry. I didn't mean to startle you."

He looked at her for a moment, then turned back. "See the one out in front with the white war shirt on? That's White-Shield-Owner."

"Their leader?"

"Yes."

"Is he the one you talked to before?"

"Yes, I've known Shield a long time. He's one of . . ."

"They're stopping, Kit."

He saw them go through the same maneuver they had gone through before. He bent and rested one hand on the wagon tongue. "You stay here, and if Lige comes back tell him . . . by God . . . to shoot the next idiot that fires a gun."

"Where are you going?" Her smoke-gray eyes were like agate, clear and sharp and very wide.

"Council. They want to talk."

"They'll kill you. Kit . . . no!"

He leaped the tongue and threw her an annoyed look. "Don't be a . . . a . . . woman," he said, then started forward where the resplendent figure was sitting his horse, waiting.

There was a taller, younger, more massive and powerfully built war leader beside White-Shield-Owner. Kit didn't recognize him until they were close, then he knew him by the squinting, intensely peering look he wore. Big Eagle.

His heart sank. Big Eagle didn't belong to White-Shield-Owner's band. That meant—he groaned—the smoke signal the night before had been answered. There were two bands out there now.

"*How kola, mita koda*," Big Eagle called in a booming voice. "*Wasichu, mita koda*!"

Kit grinned, but it was an effort. He had sense enough not to wear so palpably false a smile, and let it die. "How are you, my friend?" he called back, echoing what the big warrior had said. "It's been a long time."

"*Owgh*! White-Shield-Owner told me you were here. What kind of a fool are you, anyway? Those *wasichus* are doomed. White-Shield-Owner still has over ninety men of war. I brought another eighty."

They all squatted. Beyond the war leader and White-Shield-Owner—who was a peace leader (although thirty years before he had been a great fighter)—were row upon row of painted, decorated, and heavily armed *ozuye we' tawatas.*

"Big Eagle, hear me. Your medicine is strong. Your heart is as good as White-Shield-Owner's heart. Let the *wasichus* pass through. What can they hurt? What harm do they do?"

"*Owgh*! It can't be, Ohiyesa," the rumbling voice said slowly. "They have no right here. I could slit every throat among them myself. We are fighting a hard war, *koda*."

"You can't win it," Kit said firmly.

Big Eagle's squinted eyes watered continually. It gave him a fishy expression. "We *are* winning it."

"But for how long, Big Eagle? I told you that two years ago when we were hunting. The white people are too many."

"They are your people."

"Yes, but I'm not blind. I see the wrong, but I am only one man. There isn't anything I can do."

White-Shield-Owner leaned forward and rested his forearms on his upper legs. "Have they lost many, Ohiyesa?"

"More than they should have," Kit admitted candidly.

"Then they aren't as good at fighting as we are," Big Eagle said.

Kit shrugged. "I don't think so, either. That doesn't matter, Big Eagle. If you kill five, twenty more spring up in their place. If you run off fifty of their horses, the next band brings a hundred in their place. You know this is true."

"What should we do, then?" Big Eagle asked angrily. "Should we bow our heads like old women? Pull the blanket over our heads and made a death chant? No! It is better that we die strong and free than live weak and in slavery."

"You wouldn't be slaves, Big Eagle."

"No? The white man makes the black man his slave. Why wouldn't he treat the red men the same way? No, Ohiyesa, we will fight. There is no other way. We have always fought. Everything fights. There is no such thing as peace. It is a vision . . . nothing more. Why are men born lean of flank like a cougar and deep of chest like a bear? To fight! The strong live off the weak. If you whip me, Ohiyesa, or if your race whips my race, someday there will come another man stronger than you. Another race stronger than your race. It is always like that. That is life. It was decided long ago that men should live like that."

Big Eagle's moist, weak eyes shone with an inner fierceness. His nostrils expanded like an angry stallion's nostrils. Kit could see how worked up he was. He remained silent, not out of fear but because he couldn't find it in his heart truthfully to disagree.

White-Shield-Owner bent farther forward. His old face was wrinkled and yet a light showed in it. "*Owgh*!" he grunted. "It is as he says, Ohiyesa. You know it as well as I do."

"You don't believe in war," Ohiyesa reminded the old chieftain.

"In fighting, yes. In this kind of a war, no. This is annihilation, Ohiyesa. For one or the other it is extermination. I don't believe in that, but in fighting . . . yes."

It was too abstract for Kit. He went back to the original conversation. "For the people down there in the wagon train this is survival. By fighting them you weaken the Ogallalas, not the whites."

Big Eagle waved a brawny arm wide, in a great circle. "If these pass, then there will be whites behind us as well as in front, Ohiyesa. We will be surrounded. After that we will be crowded. After that . . . wiped out. Take them back. When White-Shield-Owner told me you were with them, I wanted to talk to you. The warriors don't want to talk. They say kill you, too. You are white. You are now our enemy. All whites are our enemies. I said no. You and I are old friends. We have ridden side-by-side against the Snakes. We are brothers. Take them out of this country, Ohiyesa."

When Big Eagle said the last sentence, his tone dropped. It indicated the council was at an end. Kit wanted to say a hundred things. He had lived with these men. Their life had been his for years.

He said nothing. There was no way to bridge the abyss. He got up very slowly and watched them stand. He could see in their faces that they knew already what his answer was. Then he shook his head.

"I can't."

There was no look of enmity in any of the three faces. Kit turned and started back. His heart was like lead. He felt as though something great and strong and warm had been taken bodily out of him.

He didn't look back until he was within the circle again, where the people, silent, thronged around him, staring. Lige alone understood. He made a path through them. Wooden-faced, Kit walked far to the north end of the circle and told Lige what had been said. Some of his own brooding melancholy showed in Lige's face. They stood apart for a while, watching the emigrants break up into little groups, talking, then Kit shoved upright and jerked his head.

"Let's go, Lige. The past's ended. I don't reckon I'll ever hate seeing anything pass again, as much as I do those days."

They went back among the emigrants. The sun was hot and just a little off-center. A hundred questions were asked. Kit answered every one as best he could with great patience, then the men went back to their barricades, and Kit was left standing beside Allie.

She saw the pain in the background of his eyes. "You *do* like them, don't you?"

"Yes. It's hard not to. You don't know, Allie. You'll never know. It's all past now."

"I'm sorry," she said softly.

"You won't be in a little while. There are two bands out there now. Not just White-Shield-Owner's band, but another band under Big Eagle."

"More warriors?" she asked, almost in a whisper.

He answered, looking moodily at the people hurrying busily around the compound, not wanting to see her face.

"Yes."

"Oh, Kit."

"It could be worse," he said savagely. "It could be five bands."

He walked over, where the men were getting settled. There was perspiration running along his ribs under his shirt. It tickled. “You’re fighting for survival now, fellows. Not victory . . . survival.”

“Kit!”

He knew from the urgency in Lige’s voice what it was, but he didn’t move any faster. At the break between the wagons he saw them coming. Slowly, horses at a walk, an awesome wall of them, nearly two hundred strong, the craftiest, most courageous men of war on the plains.

He saw the war honors braided into their hair and into the foretops, manes, and tails of their horses. Every man was a coup-counting, seasoned fighting Indian. Behind him were seventy-odd emigrant men with no knowledge of what they faced and even less experience as fighters.

He turned, shot Lige a sardonic smile, and spoke. “There’s the end of the trail, old horse. Take a long look.”

“*Owgh*! Don’t like the looks of Dakotas from in front . . . never did.”

A bronze figure, naked to the waist, with the sun glancing off his greased skin like old gold, walked forward with a red-stone pipe in one hand, a naked knife in the other. He stopped his horse with knee pressure, raised the calumet high so that it shone blood red, and cried out a lashing harangue. Then he threw the peace pipe down with terrible violence. It broke into a dozen pieces. The warrior ranks behind the speaker howled in thunderous approval.

Next, the war leader lifted the knife and stormed at the watching white people in his keening chant and flung the knife, too. It spun end over end and stuck quivering amid the ruin of the stone pipe.

Kit waited for no more. He turned and cupped his hands around his mouth. “Get back where you belong, dammit!”

The people reacted as though he had struck them. Their faces were pale but their eyes burned. The men were grimmer, more silent now than they had been since he had first ridden out of Independence with their train.

“What did he say?”

Her smoke gray eyes were dry and unmoving on his face. He scowled at her. “Tell you another day, Allie. Get into a wagon and lie flat. Cover up and stay put. They’re coming now. It’s all over but the shooting.”

Chapter Seven

When the Dakotas came, they were bunched up. Kit watched them in the pall of terrible silence that drenched the countryside. He saw the big buck with the naked chest ride out in front. He could tell from the *tvibluta* (sign talk) gestures that the warriors were being split into two attacking groups. His heart sank when he saw the men of war ride off slowly, a little apart, and stop. Behind them was what he had feared there might be. A solid rank of no less than sixty rock-hard, veteran shock troops.

"Lige!"

The older man trotted up, took a long look, and smothered an oath. "Three sides at once."

"Yeah. Go over on the south side and settle the men there. I'll make the north side, then come back here."

They hurried, each with his heart beating fast. Kit found the defenders hunkering like statues, only their eyes watching. He explained what was going to happen, then ran back where his own shock troops were lying.

Just as he got close, the Dakotas raised the yell. The sound was blood-chilling. Kit dropped low and shot a quick look around the front of a wagon. The Indians were breaking out in a wild race. The north and south wings of their force were veering off. He riveted his glance on the core of bunched-up, head-on warriors. They were swinging closer and closer.

He ducked under the wagon and saw the strained, oily, sweating faces of his men. "Steady!" he shouted over the scream of the Indians. "Hold on!"

The attackers were well within range now, coming faster, more compactly, as though to bowl over the wagons themselves. Kit drew his pistol, cocked it with a slippery thumb, and raised it. His breath was hot and dry in his throat. Closer. . . .

"Fire!"

The roll of gun thunder, the wreathing of unclean gray-white smoke, and the wild screams of men and horses made a din so terrible even Kit was appalled by it.

"Reload!"

The spattering gunfire north and south of them ate into the ringing echo of their own fire. Indian yells broke over the bedlam and emigrants' screams answered back.

In front of them was a sickening welter of men and horses. The painted war symbols, the metal accoutrements, the vivid splashes of scarlet flung wildly over the entire scene made the carnage an unnerving thing to look upon.

Behind the shattered front rank the other warriors had to break and fight their way around both ends of the jumble. Kit swore a grateful prayer, and bitter exultation raced through him like wine. "Shoot, dammit! Make every shot good . . . and shoot!"

The emigrant men, like veterans, until you saw the seared, blanched illness in their faces, moved with fumbling fingers. They picked out individual Indians and fired at will. The staccato blasting of their gunfire made a ragged tapestry of noise against the red wall of Dakotas and their horses. The first assault had been broken but the fight went on as viciously as before except that now the Indians, with their ranks shattered and seeing they couldn't get into the circle, either rode, streaking low, to join the north or south flanks of their army, or threw themselves flat behind the mound of men and horses and waged individual, dueling warfare.

Kit had time to see that the siege had only begun. Someone was standing outside the wagon, calling his name. He looked down the row of defenders with a bleak feeling of bitter kinship. "Don't waste a shot, boys," he said loudly. "Make damn' sure." Then he squirmed out and peered up into the countenance of the fiery-faced man named Reaves.

"Kit . . . there. They're coming through!"

Reaves was pointing. His face was like clay and his pointing arm shook. Inside the circle was a screaming band of warriors. Only one was still on his horse and even as Kit looked, the man fell sideways with a startled look. Through the dust he saw there was no danger. The Indians were hemmed in by emigrants. He heard Lige's war cry rise like a wolf wail, then die off into little coughing barks. The Indians were fighting almost back to back. The muffled crash of handguns pressed against bronze bodies was eloquent. If the men of war had gotten support from their companions, it might have been different. They didn't and their numbers dwindled even as Kit watched. He let out an uneven, withheld breath and turned to Reaves with a harsh stare.

"When you see something like that . . . fight! Don't come running to me!"

He turned and trotted toward Lige, leaving Reaves, shaken and badly frightened, to stare after him. He passed two women, lugging a heavily bearded man who groaned through lips that worked and contorted in the dark shrubbery of his face. One of the women was Allie. Their eyes met as he went past, calling to Lige.

The mountain man stood up and began reloading his pistol without glancing up. Kit threw a quick look where the Indians had been. They were no longer upright. He turned his back, ignoring the triumphant shouts of the emigrants who were as thick as flies by their carcasses.

"Just one breakthrough, Lige?"

"Yeah. If they'd come together, it would have been enough, too." Lige holstered his gun. "Damn!

That was close. Must've been a few glory hunters who had an idea of their own."

"Can you spare about five men to watch the east side?"

"I reckon. I'll get five more from the north side. That's enough, I guess. If they watch their shots, it'll be more'n enough." Lige looked up with a sudden grin and big wag of his head. "They can fight, Kit. By granny, they can fight after all."

"No choice now," Kit said somberly. "Pass the word they'll besiege us now . . . or something."

But the Dakotas didn't. They used the fire-arrow strategy. They sent a swirl of hard-riding, hard-shooting warriors in close to the circle. These were between the defenders and Indians who came next, on the far side of the howling red men. The latter warriors were armed with three fire arrows apiece. Kit and Lige both saw what was coming at the same time and hollered out as loud as they could for the women to man the water buckets.

The warning came none too soon. Fire arrows—regular war arrows but with tufts of dry grass or moss bound loosely to their arrowheads—came looping high, aimed at the vulnerable canvas of the wagon tops.

Some of the men ran, cursing, to help put out the fires. The dust was bad enough. The smoke made it stifling, although no serious damage was sustained by the emigrants.

After that the Indians drew off and Kit went more objectively among the people he captained. There were—miraculously—no dead and only six wounded. He took heart. Lige was talking to Reaves when he found him.

"Reaves, get the women to make some gruel or something. We'll eat where we lie and in relays. Organize it like that." He turned his back on the emigrant. Reaves hurried off. "Lige, I've got a notion. Tonight I'm going to take thirty men or so, get you to scout up where the devils are hiding, and hit 'em hard."

Lige, thinking in terms of defense only, was astonished. His eyes bulged but, typically, he said nothing until he rolled it over a few times in his mind, then he nodded grudgingly. "It might worry 'em a little."

"It'll do more'n that, if what I've got in mind works."

"What's that?"

"Hunt me up around sundown. I'll show you."

The women responded quickly. The smell of food grew strong in the air. And the Indians came back in a thundering blur of horsemen so no one got to eat for a long time. The rattle of gunfire punctuated every ebb and flow of enemy riders. Kit watched them, trying to surmise what they would do next. The frontal charge had been broken. Fire arrows hadn't worked. But the Dakotas were a long way from giving up and he knew it.

Another split charge past the wagons, another deafening din of musketry, and the plains fighters whipped westward again, reined up just out of rifle range, dismounted, and began to cool out their excited, lathered horses. They walked them up and down, back and forth. Kit watched the war leaders assemble a little apart from the bucks, squat, and hold a council. One man in particular held his attention. It was the muscular Dakota with the bare torso. He was angry. It showed in the tense way he leaned and in the furious ways he gestured.

Kit turned away and looked around the bedraggled circle.

Several emigrant animals had been killed. Men were dragging the dead Indians to a gap between wagons and throwing them outside. Lige was talking to a rusty-headed, tall, gaunt youth. Someone was walking toward Kit, head high, smoke-gray eyes and black hair shining. Allie.

"Here. It isn't much but it's hot."

It was a crockery bowl with barley soup in it. He looked from the spoon to her face, carefully removed the implement, tipped up the bowl, and drained it. Then he smiled. It beat a warm path all the way down to his stomach. Made him feel better almost instantly.

"That's another white man habit I think the Indians have a better substitute for. Anything you don't chew, you drink."

She smiled. "It doesn't really matter, I suppose, out here."

"Back in Independence it wouldn't look very good, would it?"

The smile lingered but turned rueful at the mental image of this tall, lean man with the ruffled blond hair standing, wide-legged, in a hotel dining room, drinking soup with his head thrown far back. "No, I don't suppose it would," she said. "How did the pioneers do, this time?"

"Much better," he said drawlingly. "You know, I think if they live through this, they just might be able to scratch a way in this country. Did your paw make it all right?"

She nodded. "Yes, Dad's all right. Mother lost some dishes and things."

He was on the verge of clucking sarcastically, but stopped the impulse in time.

"What are they doing now?" She was gazing out over the plain.

"Trying to figure out what to do next." He twisted and gazed at the far line of warriors and the squatting leaders. He shrugged. "Hard to say what's next. They've still got a bag of tricks."

"Those fire arrows were frightening. It's fiendish . . . the way they fight, I mean."

He looked back at her and made a slight motion with one hand. "We won't argue about that right now. Are you getting used to the sight of blood and bodies?"

She nodded gravely. “I won’t ever get used to them, but as long as they’re Indian bodies, I don’t mind very much.” She saw the drag and seamed look of his face. “You’re tired, aren’t you?”

“Well, I got to thinking last night and plumb forgot to sleep.” He said it with a smile, his glance going over her face slowly, softly. “Lots to think about.”

She shied away from the look in his eyes. “It’ll be sundown in another hour or so. I hope they wait until tomorrow to fight us anymore.”

“Me, too,” he said, looking back out to where the Dakotas were. “And they just might. See those bucks mounting up? Well, they’ll either head down here or back where they came from, up there on the south slope.” He smiled grimly. “It’s a cussed good thing the grass is green and wet. They’d burn the prairie otherwise.” He looked around at her again. “Maybe we’ve got a chance, after all, ma’am.”

The Indians had had enough. Kit and Lige both knew it when they saw them streaming slowly back the way they had come. Lige spat grimly over a wagon tongue. “Be as dark as it’s going to get in another hour or so, boy. You still got your scheme?”

“Yeah. Let’s go round us up some horses and riders. This has got to work out just right, Lige, or these folks’re goners.”

“I know,” Lige said softly. “You take about half

the effective fighting force out of the circle, Kit, and you're taking an awful gamble with these people's lives."

They were walking up where men were lying flat, resting. Their footsteps were soft on the dusty ground, but the sounds they made carried. After the hideous racket of the long day, the smaller sounds were like strangers to those who heard them.

"Lige," Kit said very soberly, "if we don't do something to discourage those men of war, they'll keep us bottled up here forever. What I'm afraid of . . . but don't tell these people . . . is that they'll send for more reinforcements. It's a bad gamble, but we've got to get the train moving. If we don't, we're doomed sure as the devil."

"Hadn't figured that," Lige said slowly. "I believe you're right, Kit." He flagged with a thick arm. "There's four of the best 'uns I had under the wagons today."

"Go get them. I'll hunt up the rest. Meet me down where the horses are as soon as you can. Don't tell anyone what we're up to."

Kit picked his men carefully. The first ones chosen were the emigrants he had noticed as being the coolest under fire. He sent them down to the north end of the circle and detailed the rest of the men to guard duty.

Lige had eleven men when Kit got down there. They were saddling horses and hardly speaking.

Gray-faced, sunken-eyed, and weary, there was still fight in them. Lige watched Kit come up with a questioning look. He said nothing.

Kit motioned the men close to where he stood. Looking into their dirty faces, he found a lot of weariness but no defeat. That was what he was looking for. "All right boys. Get on your horses and follow me. When we're beyond the wagons, I'll tell you the rest."

They worked fast. Mounted, they were a hard-looking crew. Guns bristled like icicles under the weakest of moonlight. Kit led them through a ready-made opening Lige had thoughtfully provided, and, once outside, he turned his horse and stopped, facing them.

"Lige, pick a couple of the best and scout ahead for sentries. There'll be a couple, at least, down in the valley. After you've taken care of them, give the coyote call. We'll wait, out a ways."

Lige peered into the faces until he found two iron-eyed men that he'd noticed during the day. Then he smiled wolfishly and beckoned them forward. His words were crisp and curt. Kit only heard part of what he said before the men were beyond hearing. "Muffle the sounds of your spurs, boys. Slide the guns down so's the barrels are in your stirrups. No reflection that way. No, dammit . . . behind your leg . . . that's it. Now, not a sound and we'll . . ."

Kit turned back to the others. "I didn't tell you

what I want to do before because I didn't want the women to know we'd be gone for a while, and maybe get scairt to death. Dakotas don't fight at night. I know it and now you do, too, but I reckon convincing the women'd be pretty hard. Now, we're going to find their camp and put 'em afoot."

Someone made a muffled gasp. Kit squinted for the man but couldn't find him. It was misty dark with a filter of weak light. A good night, in many ways.

"The main thing is not to make any noise. Those of you who have spurs, throw them away or wrap rags around them . . . something, anyway, so's there'll be no spur music. Keep your pistols holstered and put your rifles behind your legs. If you've got metal hatbands, take 'em off. Everything that'll make a noise or reflect light, shuck it or cover it. Do it now, while I'm watching."

The men went to work. Kit watched with a cold smile. They were learning fast. When the coyote call came, eerie and soft, he beckoned with his hand. "Let's go. Don't talk and do what you're told. No questions . . . plenty of time for talking afterward."

They rode slowly, seeking the deepest shadows, until a man on a horse loomed up so suddenly out of the night that Kit's heart lurched. It was one of Lige's scouts. He looked grim when Kit rode in beside him. "We got three of 'em, but Lige says we'd best go south and hug the forest for there's sure to be more on the peaks around us."

Kit nodded and reined away. They found Lige waiting for them with a rueful expression. He was bent low in his saddle, massaging a knee.

"One get you, Lige?"

"No, damn it. When he fell, I got tangled up in his legs some darned way and fell on a rock."

Kit grinned. They rode south and picked up the other scout. After that, they kept steadily across the valley until the deep, inky darkness of the forest's fringe engulfed them. There, Kit reined up. "Go ahead, Lige. We'll leave the horses here and follow."

Lige took his two men and went ahead on foot. They were lost to sight almost instantly. Kit motioned two older men forward. His voice was low. "Stay here and guard the horses. Keep your eyes open, too, or you might never see another daylight." Without waiting, he led the rest of the men along the fringe of trees in Lige's path.

They went a good long quarter of a mile before they found one of Lige's men. He was standing so close beside a tall fir tree they didn't see him until he moved. Instantly two score guns had him lined up and icy fingers were hooked tensely around triggers. "Christ," the man said hoarsely, "it's darker'n the inside of my hat." He saw Kit looking at him and bobbed his head. "On up the way. He left me here. . . ."

"I know. Stay here. Let's go."

The men strung out around him in a weaving shadow of darkness. They went as softly as they could, and the trees aided in muffling sounds so well that by the time they found the second man, he was more startled by them than they were by his rising silhouette as he came off his haunches.

"Whoo! Scary out here. He went on an' told me to stay here." The glistening eyes looked straight at Kit. "That right?"

"Right as rain," Kit said. "Come on, boys."

He kept walking until an owl hooted up in the trees, then he spun quickly and, motioning without a sound, threw himself facedown. The emigrants needed no further urging; they went down like pole-axed steers. Kit could feel the sweat break out under his shirt. He lay perfectly still, waiting, his heart thumping tightly.

The owl hoot came again, closer. Kit raised his head, listened, then drew in a breath and hooted back. The wait wasn't long after that. Lige materialized out of the firs like a wraith. He sidled down to Kit and dropped on his haunches. His face was shiny and his eyes burned with a strange light.

"I found 'em, all right. They've got guards out, but, hell . . . they're sleeping better'n the rest. They sure figure those emigrants're bottled up and harmless."

"Where's the camp?"

"About a half mile through the trees. There's a little valley over there."

"Good. The horses?"

Lige smiled widely. "That's even better," he said. "They got 'em all on this side of the meadow with two more guards."

Kit twisted his head and looked into the glowing eyes of the emigrant behind him. "Go back where we saw our last man. Take him with you and trail back where the first fellow was. All three of you go back where the horses are and bring 'em up here."

The man got up very slowly, turned, and started back along the trees without a word. Kit swung back to Lige. "Look like they've got any new bucks in with 'em?"

"No. The same two bands as near as I could make out. Sleeping like logs, too. They figure that, outside of you and me, those whites are bogged down in fear, hiding behind their wagons, scairt to death."

"Damned good thing they figure things like that, Lige." Kit sat up and crossed his legs under him and watched the other men do the same. "Did you see any other sentinels out?"

"Didn't see any, Kit, but from the edge of their meadow you can see a bony peak that's behind the trees. They can see the wagon train from up there so I expect there's a buck watching from there."

"How do we get to him?"

"Follow right through the trees here. Smack the way you're facing. Due south and a mite west.

Don't you want me to stick around and guide you in?"

Kit shook his head. "No. We'll come a-horseback and bring your animal, Lige. You go back and keep an eye on 'em. If they've got sentinels above the valley, they might've seen us moving. You watch and see if anyone comes trotting in to waken 'em. If not . . . fine. If a sentry *does* come, do all the horse damage you can, then run like hell back here."

Lige got up. His leathery face still had the same sheen of excitement to it. "I'll be looking for that horse, boy. Hate like hell to have to try and outrun some of those long-geared bucks at my age, afoot."

Kit nodded soberly and watched Lige melt back into the forest again. He explained what was next while he waited for the horses to come up. The emigrants grunted soft questions and Kit could tell from their faces that most of their uneasiness was gone and a tingling excitement had taken its place.

Chapter Eight

When the horses came, they mounted and followed Kit into the forest. The darkness was complete, then. A brooding, vast blackness steeped in a frightening silence.

Kit rode with a worried feeling that some of the emigrants might become separated from the others among the trees. When Lige appeared suddenly at his stirrup, he looked down at him. The old mountain man made the sign-talk sign for dismount. Kit swung down and leaned toward his partner.

"Right ahead. See yonder where there's a little gray light beyond the trees? Well, that's where the meadow is. If you go any farther with the horses, the danged Indian critters'll smell 'em and nicker, maybe."

Kit handed Lige his reins and went forward afoot, without a sound. When he got to the edge of the trees, he peered out. The camp smells of men and animals and cooking fires hung in the air. The horses were between him and the distant, obscure mounds that were sleeping warriors. He ducked back and hurried to where Lige was holding Kit's reins and the reins of his own horse. "Lige, it couldn't have been better if we'd made it that way."

"I know. How you want to do it? Hit the herd, then ride over the bucks?"

"No." Kit shook his head. "Just the horses. Hit 'em hard and fast like the Indians do, and push 'em back out into the valley as fast as we can. Don't bother to fight. Just get their horses."

Lige nodded. "Want me to tell the boys?"

"We both will."

They rode among the emigrants and explained the strategy. None dissented although two were reluctant to let the Dakotas off so cheaply. Kit explained to them that setting an Indian afoot was worse than death anyway. The warrior not only had the shame and humiliation to bear, he also had to walk through miles of hostile country to get back to his village.

They went all the way to the edge of the forest before an Indian horse nickered. The sound didn't carry very far. It was the soft call of a horsing mare. Kit tightened in his saddle and reined as far south of the herd as he dared. Not until he was coming out of the trees did he see the Indian standing as erect and suspicious as a piece of lean, dark wood, staring at the mare that had called. He was raising his gun when the Indian must have heard an iron shoe strike a rock. He whirled like a panther, squatting low, his carbine held in both hands.

"*Hit 'em!*"

Three guns exploded at once. The Indian went

over backward under the impact of lead. He rolled against a lightning-shattered stump and lay there. The emigrants knew how to herd horses if they didn't know how to fight their owners. They hit the herd in a rolling mass of human and horseflesh and never stopped. Several raised the yell.

Kit saw Lige whirl past. He held his horse back under a fretting rein and watched the encampment. Warriors came rolling out with cries of consternation and fury, their voices hoarse. Kit watched the emigrants under Lige's leadership sweep the Dakota horse herd down through the trees in a reckless plunge.

The Indians threw shots into the forest and broke into screams of fury. Understanding came slowly to their sleep-drugged minds. Kit lifted his revolver and fired four times as fast as he could thumb back the dog, then he followed his companions through the forest.

The unexpected fury of the shots threw the Dakotas into a scramble. They raced for cover among the trees to the east of the little glade and Kit never once looked back. All his efforts were bent on getting out of the forest safely.

When the valley floor showed ahead, he reined up once more and listened. The shouts were distant but pursuing. He eased his animal out again and loped down across the silvery grass, searching for the moving blur that would be Lige and the Dakota horses.

The howls of the men of war could be heard even after Kit caught up with the others. Full comprehension came slowly, but it came. The Dakotas were beside themselves with rage. Lige turned a shiny face with a livid grin on it. His wolf call came up out of his throat with a high, staccato sound and died away in the guttural, coughing barks. Then he laughed and the weak light shone off his teeth.

"Done it, son," he chortled to Kit. "We done it, by granny . . . and with emigrants so cussed green they smell like grass."

"Hold it for the hole in the circle, Lige," Kit said. "Plenty of time to crow later."

They ran the horses almost all the way back. When they slowed, it was to send a driving wedge of horsemen ahead to hold the excited Indian horses and slow them until they cooled enough to calm down.

The wagon circle loomed eerily, like a monstrous coiled snake, in the craggy, black-girt valley. Kit looked and felt the beauty of the scene despite the peril streaming orry-eyed behind them. The spires on both sides of the valley swept up abruptly from the plain and presented great, dark faces that seemed to frown, in the milky light, down upon the men and the forted wagons toward which they were trotting.

The moon was curled in anxiety and the sky was a shroud of purple flung over the universe like a solemn mask. Somewhere, far off, an elk trumpeted unmindful of the racket that was small and weak in the hugeness of the night—or perhaps because he was aroused by the noise. The world waited while the wild-appearing riders swung in close and threaded the snorting, half-wild Dakota war horses into the enclosure. The dust, churned up by many horses' hoofs, was like black flour in the air, on their clothing, and in their nostrils.

Kit swung down before his horse had responded to the tug. He turned on one booted foot and pointed where the gap was. "Set up that tongue and those barricades again, boys."

Only the men and women who had known that the others had ridden out came streaming, fear and relief scratched deeply into their tired faces. The first woman Kit saw was Allie Burgess. Behind her was a sturdy old man with a patriarchal beard, almost white.

"Allie," Kit said with much more calm than he felt. "You reckon you could hustle some food for the boys? They've had a mite of a ride and a trifling scare tonight. They could use food now like they never could before."

"Yes," she said, wide-eyed, searching his face for a rapt second before she went back down the circle the way she had come.

Kit stood beside his panting horse, watching the gracefully moving outline. She was tall and regal and poised even when she moved. He turned to the big old man and smiled wryly. “She’s the handsomest filly I’ve ever seen,” he said.

“Do you think so, Mister Butler?” The question was almost as mild as the look in the man’s blue eyes. It was an amused, close, wondering, speculative look.

“Yes, sir. I’ve seen white women before, a lot of ’em. Not in the past half dozen or so years, but I’ve seen ’em. Never one like that, though.”

“I’m glad you think that,” the old man said softly. “I’m sort of the same opinion. Y’see, she’s my daughter.”

Kit found his voice and balance with an effort. He swung away and left the old man standing, stockstill, looking after him. There was a blank thoughtfulness in Reuben Burgess’s face, a faint sort of doubt and dread, and wonder.

“Lige? Everybody all right?”

“Fit as a fiddle, Kit. There’s damned good horses in that bunch. We found sixteen so far that’ve got government brands on ’em.”

“No wonder they had good mounts. How many are there?”

“We must’ve lost a passel in the trees, but there’s still about a hundred-odd head. Maybe closer to a hundred and twenty. It’s a couple of times over what the emigrants’ve lost and then some.”

“Good,” Kit said, turning away. “We’ll need ’em, Lige, because we’re going to roll these cussed wagons out of here in the morning.”

He didn't see Lige's stunned look or his gaping mouth. He also didn't see Burgess walk slowly over beside Lige and stand there, looking after him.

Allie was supervising the getting of a cold meal. He raised an eyebrow at her. "Who told you not to build a fire?"

She looked up serene and confident. "No one. I just said we'd serve them cold food. It's better not to have a fire, isn't it?"

He nodded, looking at her with respect. "I underestimated you, ma'am," he said slowly.

"I did the same thing to you . . . once."

He was left with that when she moved on. It was something he took into himself and held close in an inviolate spot, then the man named Reaves came up with his weak, peevish face showing the long strain.

"How'd you do it, Kit?"

He shrugged away the admiration in the words and glance. "How are your boys on the watch, Reaves?"

"My boys? Oh, you mean us who was doing sentry watch. Oh, we're doing fine. A few of us spelled the others off. Some of us are pretty damned tired."

"I reckon," Kit said dryly. Reaves didn't get it. "Well, I'll send you the rest of the boys and you can sort of boss the guarding duty. That all right?"

Reaves showed a stain of red pleasure in his

face. “I’ll do my level best,” he said with considerable embarrassment.

Kit turned and watched the women for a while, then very slowly, with a deep frown, he walked back where the emigrant men were recounting their experience to those who had been left behind. The stories were colorful and Lige was grinning from ear to ear when Kit stopped beside him, looking with his brooding frown at the crowd of people admiring the raiders and the Dakota war horses.

“Lige, go through the men and sort out those that drive wagons. Send ’em all over here where we’re standing.”

Lige looked up quickly. “Kit. You weren’t serious.”

“Dead serious.”

“Just dead,” Lige said quickly, “if you try and move these people in the face of all those Indians.”

Kit relaxed and threw all his weight on one leg. “Listen, Lige, we took a long chance tonight. The only way we’ll get out of this mess is if we take the initiative. I mean . . . if we make the first moves and keep the Dakotas guessing.

“We were just damned lucky tonight, Kit, and you know it.”

“Call it what you want. The thing is, we crippled ’em bad, Lige. Hit ’em where it’ll hurt from now on. They’re afoot and . . .”

"Hell," Lige interrupted with a loud snort. "They'll be around here like buzzards over a bull elk's carcass from dawn on. We've just started things, Kit, not finished 'em."

"I know that," Kit said with his weariness making his control slip a little. "Let 'em come. They'd've come anyway, Lige. Now we've got the initiative and, by God, we're going to keep it. If we don't, they're going to butcher us like cattle. Now go get the drovers and send 'em back here while I hustle 'em, too."

He didn't wait for further argument but went among the talking groups of filthy people and told every man he saw that he wanted the wagon owners and drivers apart from the others. Lige did his work well. The men drifted along when Kit walked away from the horses. Lige came up with his eyes alight, steady and level on Kit's face.

"Boys, I want you to take your critters and harness up." He stopped deliberately, watching their expressions in the murky light. Astonishment spread like water among them. Kit nodded grimly. "Those of you that've had a broke horse killed, lash an Indian horse beside your good animals. Those with oxen dead, use Indian horses. When you've got 'em all ready, run a jerk line from your lead teams to the running gear of the wagon in front of you. One thing above all else will save you. Don't leave any gaps between the teams and the wagons ahead of you!"

"How about the danged Injuns?" a man called out from the rear of the crowd.

"They'll be afoot, so they won't dare come up too close, but they'll be ready to shoot whenever they get a chance," Kit said.

"Well, hell," another emigrant protested loudly. "They'll get our critters."

"I'm gambling they won't," Kit said. Then wearily: "Do like I say, boys. We can make a run for it or we can stay here and let 'em eat us up a little at a time."

Lige sided with Kit out of loyalty alone. He thought the idea was worse than madness, but on the other hand he knew, also, that staying here indefinitely was impossible.

The emigrants went shuffling back to where the women were waiting. Kit and Lige trailed in their wake, answering questions and pointing out the futility of staying where they were.

Allie saw Kit and Lige standing back and to one side of the others. She made up two tins of cold food and took them to the scouts. Then she stood silently, watching them eat. Kit worked up a wan smile and very gravely winked at her. She flushed and threw him a dark look of warning that he duly ignored.

"Allie, it's either good or I'm hungrier'n a bear."

"You're hungry," she said, "and dog tired. You look old."

"I am old," he said. "I've never felt as old in my life as I do right now."

"Ten hours of rest would fix that, Kit."

He shook his head. "No, the only thing that'll fix that, Allie, is the sight of Fort Collins from the wagon box of one of those cussed Conestogas."

"Will we ever get there, Kit?" There was a wistfulness to the way she said it that wasn't in the steadiness of her gray glance.

"Lord knows, Allie, I don't. We're going to try, though, in the morning."

"You mean . . . move out?"

He saw her face tighten. "Yes, ma'am. If we stay here, we're goners. If we move out, they may get us anyway, but at least we'll be going in the right direction. It's stand still and get scalped or run and get scalped."

She didn't speak again until they were both finished eating. Then she saw the men leading animals out, lifting harness and yokes, and rattling the coarse chain tugs. Realization came slowly. It was borne in upon her by the unmistakable activity. She turned her head slowly, seeing the grim, bitter determination in the way the men worked and in the way the women loaded up the wagons again. Her heart sank.

"Kit. . . ."

"There's no other way, Allie," he said gently. "It's run or stand. We've stood about all we dare. Now we've got to run."

She turned and walked slowly back where the other women were breaking camp. He let out a long rattling sigh and nudged Lige. "Let's get our horses. We'll want 'em to line out right at dawn."

"Kit," Lige said softly, "the Indians'll be out there, lying in the grass like pebbles."

"I know it, Lige. I know it."

They found that someone had grained their horses. There were several boys around, admiring the horse herd. Kit resaddled his horse, turning the blanket over so the sweat side was up, then mounted, and waited for Lige. A tall youth with fiery red hair came over deferentially.

"Mister Butler, sir. Do you reckon a man'd dast take a horse to ride out of what's left?"

"Have they gotten all the teams they need?"

"Yes, sir."

"Well, then, I reckon it'd be a good thing if every fellow your age among the wagons dug up a saddle and rode. As a matter of fact," Kit said, eyeing the youth, "when you've got about ten or twenty lads mounted, hunt me up, and I'll give you a job. We'll need every cussed rider we can get from here on."

The youth's face lit up with an immense smile. He watched Kit and Lige ride away, his lips moving without sound and his eyes shining damply.

"They might get hurt, Kit."

He shrugged. "Get hurt anyway, Lige, if we don't make it."

"I reckon so," Lige said morosely.

"Look at that tomfool emigrant, anyway."

Two of the Dakota horses, grotesque among the staid, colorless other animals in a wagon's harness, were bucking, pitching, and throwing themselves under the heavy, chafing chain harness. The strangeness of the white man smell and the excitement were like electricity to them.

Kit rode up beside the emigrant who was standing, wide-legged, staring. He bent low from the saddle and touched the man's shoulder.

"Pardner, you'll never get a mile like that. Split 'em up. Don't ever hitch two wild ones side-by-side. Put a tame one on the side of each wild one, then be sure your lead team's a broken pair. If you'll use your head, you'll make it." He rode away.

Lige looked back and swore. The horses had finished throwing themselves about and the tangle of the harness now was holding them down.

Kit didn't look around. "It's all right, Lige. I'd like 'em all to bust loose if they're going to. Be better here than five miles from here."

It took a long time. Kit sat like a brooding statue on his horse, watching. The sounds from the wagon circle sounded doubly loud in the dark, hushed night. Lige came riding slowly up beside him. He was chewing with rhythmic regularity.

His eyes were squinted almost closed with concern. Finally he leaned forward a little.

"Kit, they'll be strung out as helpless as babies. The Indians'll be in the grass on both sides of 'em. It'll be a slaughter."

"No," Kit said evenly. "I've got another idea, Lige. Couple more, in fact. We'll . . ."

"Mister Butler?" It was the red-headed youth. Behind him were at least twenty more youths. Guns shone dully from among them.

Kit was surprised there were so many. He smiled. "What's your name? Red?"

"That's it, sir. Red . . . Red Houston."

"Are they good men?"

Red's face glinted, flushed and eager. "Give us something to do, Mister Butler, and we'll do 'er as good as anyone could."

"All right, Red. Go among your folks and get your pockets full of whatever they've got you can eat on a long haul. Once we roll, there'll be no stopping for Lord knows how long. After that, come back here to me and I'll give you a job damn' few men could do right. Then we'll see how good you are, for sure."

Lige's eyes flickered over the boys. He spat and smiled thinly. "Looks like they'd crowd the gate of hell for you, Kit."

"It's going to take that, Lige. Maybe even more." He stood in his stirrups to see the wagons. The distance was too great and the night too dark.

He wheeled his horse. “They ought to have ’em ironed out by now, Lige. Only a little while till dawn. Let’s ride the circle and find out.”

They rode slowly, talking to men and seeing the deep, solemn questions, unspoken, in the women’s faces. Lige squirmed under the hopeful, almost prayerful looks. Kit’s face was impassive and flinty, like his eyes. Whatever he felt didn’t show until Allie Burgess came up out of the darkness and stood framed beside the immense side of a prairie schooner. She regarded him steadily with an expression almost as blank as his own. Their glances met, held, then dropped away as Kit nodded and made no move to stop. Lige looked quickly from one to the other, then followed Kit with a worried frown.

The people had their wagons loaded, their teams ready, and were waiting with a depth of desperate hopefulness for Kit, who all acknowledged as leader, to pass the next order down the line. He rode to the middle of the wagon circle and leaned forward in his stirrups, seeing the faint, pale globes that were faces. There was a painful silence. He waited until it was drawn out thin, then he turned swiftly to Lige.

“See that wagon with the fire-arrow holes in it, up ahead? The one on your right?”

“With the gray leaders?”

“Yes. Go over to that wagon, Lige, and have that fellow lead out. Wait a minute. As soon as he’s strung out of the circle, the teams behind him are to follow. Make sure they've got the teams behind them lashed to the tailgates or running gear of the wagon ahead. We don't want a space a Dakota can slip through at all." Lige was listening with a perplexed scowl.

"See the wagon just ahead of the one with the fire-arrow holes in its shroud?"

"Yeah."

"Well, have that one swing in close to your other wagon and every wagon behind him follow along."

"Make two lines, one beside the other?"

"No," Kit said with a shake of his head. "Every wagon's got to slant outward, Lige. Form the whole wagon train into a big V."

"Oh . . . hell!" Lige said, understanding flooding in. Then he began to grin. The expression grew until it almost split his face. "I'll be damned. I'd've never thought of that, Kit."

Unheeding, his eyes slitted, Kit swung an arm backward to indicate the loose stock. "The thing is, Lige, we'll have our animals protected that way. That's what the Dakotas're after right now more than our topknots. That's why I wanted that red-headed boy to mount up his friends. We'll put the cattle and horses inside the V and use those boys to close up the back end of it. See?"

"You're a regular damned medicine man, Kit. I apologize."

"Nothing to apologize for, Lige. You never said anything."

"No," Lige said slowly, "but I sure as hell was thinking a lot."

Kit turned when a rider came up beside him. It was the youth on his Indian horse. Kit explained briefly what he wanted done. Red listened, asked several questions, then dropped back to round up his friends. His face was alight with responsibility. He wore it confidently, enthusiastically, as youth always does.

"Lige, you tell the ones on your side of the wagons what we want and I'll take the other half. After that, you stay with the wagons."

"What're you going to do?"

"Take every man who can fork a horse and throw out a screen of riders across the front and down the sides of our V."

Lige fished up a plug, worried off a corner, tongued it, spat, and, throwing back his head, let out his war cry. The effect was startling. The emigrants sprang upright as though the Indians were upon them. Kit looked annoyed but said nothing. The tension showed now more than ever. He stood in his stirrups and shouted out what he wanted them all to do, then he rode toward one wagon, and Lige rode toward the one next to it.

The actual breaking up of the circle didn't take long. By dawn's first gray streaks, the V was taking shape. Men shouted at their animals and one another. The boys on their Indian horses yelled from effervescence only. They had no trouble holding the loose stock within the long wings—fifteen huge wagons long, plus from four to six teams longer. When the huge, ungainly-looking V was moving and straightening out, assuming perspective and shape, Kit dropped back and called out the riders. They came in a gray stream of horsemen. Lige rode loosely ahead of them to where Kit was waiting.

"Kit? Hell, they don't need me inside the V. S'pose I take the lead up ahead?"

"All right. Fine idea, Lige, but watch like a cussed hawk. They'll be in the grass like snakes."

"Too bad it's too green to burn," Lige said just before he rode away.

The emigrant men looked capable enough. Tired, disheveled, filthy with shiny, grease-like sweat, sunken eyes that glittered with deep resolve, and guns gripped more confidently, they were a disreputable-looking lot, but steady. It made Kit feel good to see them coming toward him like that. *Funny what adversity does to men,* he thought. *They don't even look like the same men Powers governed as wagon boss.*

"Boys, they'll be out there ahead of us. They're afoot, as you know, except for a handful of them. They'll have one advantage over you. They'll be low in the grass, shooting up. You'll be on your horses, mounted and good targets."

"We could walk," a man said roughly.

"No, you've got horses and that's better'n shelter. You can run 'em down and that's worth more than being hidden. We'll have fights right along, I'm convinced of that, but if we don't break and let 'em draw us off, we'll whip 'em. Remember that one thing. If you chase a buck, don't go more than a hundred feet or so. If he gets away, let him go. It's a damn' sight more important to guard the wagons than to kill a few Dakotas." He looked past them where the high-hooped wagons were rumbling, stirring up dust even though the dew still lay lightly on the ground. Great, cumbersome vehicles, lurching, waddling, rolling across untracked wilderness.

"Fan out across the front of the train and down the sides. We won't use much of a rear guard. There're boys back there, and if we sweep clean ahead, they won't do much damage behind us. Stay out a couple hundred feet from the wagons. The worst danger right now is the teams. Every horse or ox they down will delay us that much. That's what you're for. Protect the wagon train and don't take any chances while you're doing it. Anything that's moving in the grass, shoot." He turned his head and looked up where Lige was. "Anyone want to say anything?"

"Yeah," a bearded man with a swarthy face said. "How'll we know who's to ride where?"

Kit regarded the man for a moment before he

answered him. "Listen, mister . . . from now on you're a Westerner. You stand on your own damn' two feet and you use your God-given head. If you don't, you'll make grass grow for future generations. If you do, you won't have to ask damn' fool questions like that. Wherever you see a gap, fill in. Whenever you see an enemy, shoot. Don't wait for someone to tell you to." He swung his arm. "Half on the far side of the train, the others here. Point your half circle so's there'll be at least ten men up front, behind Lige. Let's ride!"

Kit broke away and loped up to Lige. The emigrants milled a little, then several men among them led contingents of the riders around the front of the train and down the north side.

Lige watched and looked approvingly at the scene as daylight pinkened and the diorama of their strategy showed clearly. Wagons rolling westward, outriders far away on both sides sweeping the valley, and a hard core of older men, mostly bearded and bleak-looking under their old hats, walking their horses slowly, purposefully, up where Kit and Lige sat side-by-side, studying their wagon train. "Damnedest thing I ever seen, Kit."

"Me, too. It better work, though."

"Work? Hell, it'll work all right. Only thing now is how we're going to get through the passes."

Kit nodded and lifted his reins. "That's something else. We'll sweat over that when we get there. Right now I'm thinking about Big Eagle's men of war. They'll be watching us, figuring where a weak spot is."

"There ain't a weak spot," Lige said firmly.

"Better not be."

Kit rode to meet the men who were stopped, waiting. "Do whatever Lige tells you to do, boys." Accepting their tight-mouth nods, he rode on down the skirmish line and didn't turn until he was almost behind the train. There, he could see how young Red Houston and his cohorts were effectively blocking off the escape route for the loose stock inside the V.

The entire thing was working out even better than he had hoped it would. *Survival,* he thought. *Corner a weasel and he'll fight like a grizzly. Show emigrants that they would survive only if they fought like Indians and used cover even if they had to create it, and they'd learn damn' fast.*

He went far around the back of the wide wings of the train and across to the other outriders. So far no one had seen an Indian evidently, because the only popping sounds came from long rawhide drover's whips. Still, they hadn't rolled more than a half mile.

He completed his circle and found nothing that he would alter. Riding slowly far ahead where Lige was spearheading the caravan, he swung to travel stirrup to stirrup with his partner.

"Anything yet?"

Lige shot him a squinting look. “Nope, can’t make out what they’re up to. Haven’t seen even a sentinel yet.”

“Don’t fret, Lige,” he said softly. “They won’t disappoint you.”

Chapter Nine

The sun came up and dappled them with warmth. It flung down a red banner then faded fast, unrolling its fiery carpet until the land grew dusty again.

The wagon train was rocking with unwieldy majesty in its unprecedented V shape. Sunken-eyed men, wolf-like, rode far out in front and trailed down both sides.

The Indians appeared as if by magic, when they finally came. Less than two score were astride. The rest were afoot. A long, motionless line of footmen, they stared at the strange sight. Kit snorted and jutted his chin toward them.

"If they stand and fight, Lige, it'll be the first time I ever saw 'em do it."

"They won't," Lige said. But he was wrong. Kit knew they were both wrong when the scouts far ahead drew up before the train just beyond rifle range, waiting, looking back and waiting. Kit sunk in his spurs and loped ahead. Lige was beside him.

The Indians didn't fade away as they ordinarily did. Kit scowled at them and held up his hand to stop the wagons. The soft, billowing cloud of dust came lazily up where the emigrant outriders were. Lige growled deep in his throat.

Kit swung to face him, still frowning. "More to this than we can see, pardner," he said. "Take the riders on a circle of the train. Station 'em where they were, on both sides, and make 'em stay there." He shot another long, thoughtful glance at the Dakotas. "They aren't all up there, Lige. That's to draw our attention."

Lige's voice crackled out orders. The horsemen swung in behind him, all but ten or twelve that Lige left with Kit, and made a fast, hard-riding circle. An emigrant got bucked off a Dakota horse, and as the riders swung back with the caught horse, leading it up to the emigrant who was trotting to meet them, they saw the man stop rigid, rise to his full height on his toes before he pitched over facedown in the grass. They could see the long, slender shaft sticking out of his back. With a bellow, Lige whirled and led his riders in a furious charge across the valley floor.

The Indian scouts, far ahead, leaped up wildly and turned to flee. It had been one of them, a hot-blood, who had foolishly killed the white man. Now, gunfire shattered the stillness and Indians ran as hard as they could until they were shot down.

Back a ways and quite a distance off, a large war party was shouting and running forward to help their friends. They weren't strong enough, though. The horsemen slid to a grinding halt and used their guns with terrible effect. The dismounted Ogallala Dakotas broke and fled.

"Hold it, dammit! Come back here!"

Lige's voice was like the rolling blast of a brass cannon. He was red-faced and icy-eyed. The emigrants turned back and watched the men of war streak it for the trees, with angry glares. Lige motioned for two men to take the dead emigrant back to the wagons, then he swung and shouted orders, splitting up the men and sending them around the rear of the stalled train where white faces were watching. His words were scathing and fierce, but he told them what they were to do and the men did it.

He rode back up to Kit, with a crimson stain still mottling his dark face, sent a withering stare at the watching Indians, and cursed.

Kit smiled thinly at him. "Got your dander up, didn't they? Well, let's see if they'll stand." He twisted in the saddle and waved the train forward. The cry of drovers came softly. Cattle lowed and wagons rumbled.

Kit rode slowly, hardly blinking. The Indians stood steady. When they were within rifle range, Lige held up his gun. The symbol was a warning to the Dakotas. They answered it with an angry shout and a few harmless shots. Kit reined up, looked back, and saw that the wagons were coming at their snail's pace. Dismounting, he cocked his carbine, kneeled down, took a long aim, and fired. The shot was wasted. He had thought it would be. They were within range but still too far apart for good aim.

The emigrants took their cue from Kit. Even Lige, but the old mountain man shot from his horse's back, using his left arm, crossed and rigid, as his gun rest. The shots blossomed out savagely, making snarling noises and little puffs of smoke.

The horses danced a little. Kit remounted and rode steadily forward. The Dakotas fanned out. Some of the long-range shots must have scored. They spread out in the grass, kneeling so that much of their bodies were hidden. The little band of horsemen turned abruptly and rode south, far around the outflung barrier that barred the wagon train's path.

Kit watched them closely. The Indian horsemen were the strongest, most mobile hope the Dakotas had. They certainly dared not engage in close warfare with the whites, but they were a long way from being valueless.

The routed warriors, some limping, all shiny with sweat, were coming down out of the forest far south, where they met the mounted warriors. There was a brief council. Kit couldn't see what motions they made; the distance was too great. But the horsemen swung far off and paralleled the train, riding slowly down the south side. Kit looked forward again. The majority of the Indians were low in the grass. His insides churned.

"Lige, the riders are going around behind us. Take fifteen or twenty men and . . ."

"Ten'll do, Kit. You'll need the rest." Lige spun and rode back down the line, calling out names.

Kit had an uneasy moment when he thought of the boys holding the gap behind the train's V. He sucked his mouth inward. There was nothing he could do back there. Lige would do all that could be done, anyway. He spoke to the man beside him without looking around. "Go collect all the men Lige didn't take and fetch 'em up here. Hurry, time's a-wasting."

The riders came in a fast gallop. Kit hardly gave them time to draw rein. "Follow me! We've got to scatter those men up ahead before they down some animals."

They rode, stiff and upright, in a jolting trot until they were close enough to see the smoke puffs and hear the whine of Dakota bullets. Then Kit sat deep in the saddle, drew his handgun, and leaned a little. "Let's go!"

They went boiling down the land and gave the yell. The sounds, so ludicrous, coming from men who yelled with sound and nothing else, amused Kit's iron spirit. When a Dakota raised the yell, he said something, called on his medicine or his forefathers or imitated the battle cry of some animal. Not the emigrants. They just yelled to give relief to the passion and fright within them.

The Indians started shooting when the hard-riding horsemen were still a long way off. Kit squinted against the sunlight and rode with pistol balanced, cocked and ready, but unfired.

At the last moment before the emigrants started firing at the wavering bucks, Kit threw back his head and screamed like a wounded cougar. The cry had an awful lilt to it, a rising and falling crescendo of sound that shivered in the air. Then it was lost in the smash of guns and the howls of men, both red and white.

The Dakotas couldn't hope to stand before the mounted men but they stood as long as they dared, to Kit's amazement. Indians never fought pitched battles. It wasn't their way. They took honors from ambush and surprise and wily strategy. Head-on, stubborn battling seemed more than ridiculous to them; it seemed a suicidal waste of good fighting men.

Big Eagle and White-Shield-Owner's foot soldiers were no different, especially in the face of the onrushing horsemen. They shot guns and arrows, but two things saved Kit's outfit from casualties. They were riding fast and swerving erratically. The Dakotas finally broke and fled, shooting, when they shot at all, in hesitating seconds when they would stop, whirl, fire, and run on at top speed for the distant forest.

Once they broke, the Dakotas were lost. With savage fury Kit hurled his men upon them. Where a few warriors would band together and stand firm, chanting their death songs, he swung wide and left them alone. By-passing pockets of resistance, he concentrated on the single men, riding them down, and shooting them like prairie dogs.

When the wagons showed well within range, he led his blowing horse and wild-eyed emigrants back to clear out the little nests of warriors who refused stubbornly to be routed. The slaughter continued under the hot sun until the valley floor was covered with dead and dying Dakotas. None had gotten close enough to kill the harnessed animals that came on, heads high, snorting softly, smelling the blood of white man and red man, but under the firm and experienced hands of the drovers.

Kit rode back at the head of the emigrants with a savagely pleased look. Lige came loping up to meet him. He, too, was grinning like a death's head.

"We ought t' have a big powwow dance, Kit."

"Where'd the riders go?"

"Oh, they were sly ones, boy. They were going to ride plumb around in back and come up on the loose stock. Then they saw them boys, and by that time I was down there with the men. They walked, their blamed horses almost within shooting range . . . but not quite . . . and that's where they were during your fight up front."

"No danger? No lost stock?"

"Nope."

"Good. I don't think they'll recover from that skirmish right away, Lige. Want to eat?"

Lige shook his head. "Naw. You go ahead. I'll go up front and line 'em out like before, down both sides, and keep the train rolling. See you later."

Kit turned and looked at the emigrants. "Every third one of you come on. We'll see what we can scare up for food. The rest of you take your stations on both sides of the train. When we're through eating, we'll come out and relieve you."

He rode around the wagons and up behind the young men who were closing the open end of the V. Red Houston reined over beside Kit with an eager excitement, like red paint, in his face.

"Mister Butler . . . you reckon I could go out with the men?"

Kit shook his head. "Red, you couldn't serve anywhere better'n you're serving here. Honestly, you'll see that, after a while."

The boy fell back and Kit's blood-shot-eyed group rode up in among the wagons. Faces appeared as if by magic from around the great, canvas-covered bows and over tailgates. The animals within the V were grazing as they went. Kit saw Allie waving to him. She was sitting on the high seat of the seventh wagon down, on the south side. He rode over, swung onto the seat, and held the reins to his horse. Reuben Burgess nodded gravely, silently at him. He caught a glimpse of an older woman deep within the wagon but had no time for a second look.

Allie squeezed over beside her father, who gave way a little, making room for Kit. "You've done it again, haven't you?"

He saw the clear sparkle in her eyes and looked past her to the distant outriders. "No, we haven't done much, Allie. Just pushed 'em away for a little while is all."

"If we can keep that up a few days longer, we'll be safe."

He grinned sardonically. "If," he said with dour emphasis. He looked out around the seat where a purple notch in the far hills was looming closer. "See that gap, Allie?"

"Straight ahead?"

He nodded at her. "Yep. If we get through there, it'll be the miracle of the ages, ma'am."

"What's on the other side?"

"Well," he said softly, "if we get over that pass, we'll be safe, like you say . . . only I wouldn't give much for our chances."

Allie's father was studying the jagged spires that girded the trail far ahead. "Have you ever been through there, Mister Butler?"

"Kit. Yeah, twice. Once exploring . . . once in a hurry with some Rees behind me."

"Is it steep? That'd slow us badly, if it's steep."

"It isn't the steepness," Kit said, staring up at the forbidding spires. "It's the narrowness."

"Too narrow for wagons like these?"

"I didn't mean that. No, I'd say that pass has been used for hundreds of years. The trail's good. Not very steep and there's only one ford, and that doesn't amount to much, even in the spring. What I was thinking about was the sides of the pass. The wagons'll have to go through there single file. One behind the other, you see. We'll be at the mercy of the Indians. They can get on both sides and shoot down on us." He didn't say any more although a picture was formed in his mind very clearly of what would happen.

Allie and her father were looking somberly ahead. He turned and looked at the girl's profile. It was a thing he would carry inside his head always. Clean and wholesome and strong-looking, without too much prominence to any one feature. A beautiful head and a handsome face, any way he looked at it. He sighed. The sound was lost in the grinding overture from the huge wheels. Then she turned and caught him staring. He didn't drop his glance, either.

"Ma'am, you reckon you could take pity on a hungry man?"

She laughed as much with relief as with pleasure. He looked so doleful and dirty and exhausted. "Stay here for a minute." She swung around and disappeared behind the high seat, down the shadowy interior of the Conestoga.

"Mister Butler."

Kit turned and studied Burgess's face. It was strong and long with the same eyes Allie had, only small in his head from perpetual squinting. "Are you pro-slaver, by any chance?"

The question startled him. He looked beyond Burgess to the nearest outrider, where the lift and fling of the land was merged with the sky. His answer came slowly because he had to plan the words. "No, I reckon not. I haven't been east of the Missouri in many years. Out here men do for themselves. They don't need slaves . . . and if they had 'em, they'd just be another mouth to feed and another scalp to save." Then he smiled. "You know, Indians say niggers don't have souls . . . that's why they're black. Not having souls there's no reason to scalp 'em. I've always figured the reason they didn't lift nigger wool was because they couldn't get a good hold of it."

Burgess didn't speak. He looked straight ahead where the distant hills were.

Kit tried again. "I don't suppose it's right for one man to own another. Honestly we don't think much about things like that out here."

"Then you aren't a slaver?"

"No."

Burgess drove in silence for a while. He didn't speak again until Allie came back with a thick crockery plate with cold buffalo tongue on it, some white bread, and a big, quivering blob of some dark red preserves. Kit was looking his gratitude at the daughter when the father spoke.

"Is Fort Collins beyond that pass?"

Kit spoke around the food he was eating. "Beyond the pass is a big plain. It drops downward for a long way. We'll make good time if we get there. Across the plain is Fort Collins. Maybe another week's traveling."

"Then our remaining danger is the pass."

Kit ate hungrily and scowled a little. "That's taking a lot for granted, Mister Burgess," he said. "Even if we make the pass, there's still the chance they'll keep after us out on the plains. They're pretty hard to discourage, those Dakotas. When you see 'em all just turn and start riding away . . . or walking away . . . you'll know we're safe. Until then, don't take anything for granted."

"You know them pretty well, don't you?"

"I've lived with 'em, gone raiding against their enemies with 'em, hunted and feasted and sat around and jawed with 'em."

"And . . . you like them?"

"Yes." He handed the plate back to Allie and smiled his thanks. "You people don't know them. You don't understand them. All you see is war paint. Well, I reckon the best way to show you how they feel is to ask how you'd feel if the Confederates back East were to invade the

States and drive all you Federalists from your homes."

"There's a difference," Burgess said in an ominously cold way.

"No difference at all," Kit said bluntly. "They've been here too long to welcome any kind of an invasion."

"They've never worked the ground, Mister Butler. They're savages."

Kit could feel his face reddening. "Savages? Mister Burgess, they think *we're* savages. I reckon a good example of the difference between us would be this. I've yet to know an Indian who was a liar. I can't say as much for a white man." He pulled his horse's reins inward a little, drawing the plodding animal up beside the high seat. Burgess turned and watched him vault over into the saddle. His eyes were frosty. Allie swung over into the place Kit had vacated. She looked anxious and worried.

"When can we stop, Kit?"

"At sundown, Allie. No sense in stopping before. The only safety we can rely on is darkness . . . and we das'n't rely on that too much, but the men'll have to have some rest pretty soon or they'll be toppling over. Thanks, ma'am, I appreciate that food."

He reined away before she could speak. She watched him go with a soft and brooding look. Other men were riding back down the wings of the V. They were passed by the boy guards across the open end of wagons, and straggled leisurely back out onto the valley floor where they relieved other men who went to get some food.

Lige watched Kit approach. He was riding the point, far ahead of the train, with men strung out behind him on both sides of the wagons. He reined up and waited. When Kit caught up, they rode knee to knee for a while, studying the pass in silence, then Lige spat lustily.

"She's going to be hell in there, Kit."

Kit nodded thoughtfully. "Yeah. If we had enough men we could throw a string of 'em on both sides of the pass up in the trees and get the drop on our copper-hided friends."

"But we haven't," Lige said. He threw a worried look at Kit. "Have the emigrants got bells?"

"Yeah. I've seen 'em. We'll hold off on using the bells until we're pretty close, though, Lige."

"We'll be up there by tomorrow night, looks like." Lige began wagging his head back and forth. "The times I've been over that trail. Hell, I never thought I'd be guiding wagons over it."

Kit smiled. "The land's changing, Lige," he said. "Wouldn't surprise me to see you finish up your days farming."

"Plowing?" Lige said with a rush of horrified breath. "Me . . . plowing and seeding and all such stuff? Not on your damned life."

"Looks like that's the future out here, old-timer."

"Future, hell," Lige spat out. "Before I'll do that, I'll go to horse trading. These people are always needing new stock. Well, I'll steal from the Indians and trade to the whites, then I'll steal from the whites and trade to the Indians. A man ought to do right well like that."

"Until one side or the other catches him and closes off his wind," Kit said dryly.

"Well, what're you planning to do, then? I can't picture you scratching up the danged ground behind a yoke of oxen."

Kit was silent for a moment, his calm glance resting on the twin peaks far ahead, frowning down with stony impassiveness on the valley. "Up until a few days ago I hadn't thought much about it, Lige. Now I have. Seems to me a man ought to do pretty well just raising horses and cattle. Get himself a big block of land and put up a big log house and raise cattle and horses."

"Why such a big log house?" Lige was squinting at Kit with a suspicious, sniffing look.

Kit smiled broadly. "Well. You know how it is. A man can't just live alone."

"Oh," Lige said, without too much surprise. "I thought she was throwing stones at you. The last time I seen you ride past her, didn't either one of you look very pleased."

Kit turned and looked at his partner. "Must be your imagination, Lige. Except for arguing a little about Indians, we hit it off fine."

"Does *she* know that?" Lige asked wryly. "I think you'd better tell her. Women like to be told when they're going to get married to a man. Don't much like being surprised about things like that."

"Go to hell," Kit said quietly.

Lige let out a squeaking laugh and nodded at the frowning peaks. "I might do that, too. Maybe up ahead in that durned pass." He shrugged. "A fellow's got to go sometime, I reckon." He turned his horse with a sly look at Kit. "Did she feed you?"

"Yeah. Buffalo tongue and wild plum preserves, I think it was."

"Then I reckon she'll do that same for me. Leastways I can ask."

"She will," Kit said, then he turned quickly. "Lige, be careful what you say to her."

"Me?" Lige said, riding away. "Why, Kit, I'm surprised at you." His laughter came back softly.

Kit squirmed in the saddle and swore under his breath. Lige was all man, a man's man. He had about as much tact as a Dakota horse under a white man's harness.

Chapter Ten

Kit urged his horse up ahead far enough to be able to see the waving spring grass on all sides of the wagon train. If there were Dakota warriors hiding, he couldn't see them. He rode like that the rest of the afternoon, and a dawning suspicion began to form in his mind. The Indians weren't going to try and waylay them again on foot—at least not out in the open. He signaled for some of the emigrants to ride up toward him. When they came, he sent them out in sets of four, skirmishing far and wide, then he stayed where he was, watching. They didn't scare up a single hidden buck Indian.

By the time Lige came back, looking full in the face and secretly amused about something, he was convinced his suspicion was right. "Lige, I've got a notion . . ." He stopped there, studying Lige's beaming countenance with a slight frown. "What the hell have you been up to? Dog-gone you, Lige. Did you shoot off your lip back there to Allie?"

Lige's face assumed an injured look, but his little eyes never lost their pleased, sly look. "What were you going to say, Kit?" he asked with unruffled calm.

Kit studied Lige for a moment and stifled an urge to swear at him. He straightened in the saddle and stared hard at the peaks. “I was going to say . . . blast your soul . . . that I’ve had the country up ahead scouted and there’s not an Indian anywhere around.”

“So?”

“So I’ve got an idea that White-Shield-Owner and Big Eagle pulled them out.”

“Why?” Lige asked quickly. “Because they’re afoot?”

“That’s only part of it, I think. They all know they can’t match us when we’re mounted and they’re not. I’ve got a notion they’ve made tracks for the pass. They’ll have all day tomorrow to fort up there, then, when the train rolls between the bluffs, all hell will bust loose.”

Lige studied the mountains ahead somberly. He didn’t speak for a long time. Not until the sun was sliding far off center, then he shook himself like a dog coming out of a creek, took a short chew of tobacco and spat.

“That’s about it. Well, like I said, she’s going to be hell in there, Kit.”

Kit didn’t answer.

They finished out the rest of the late afternoon riding side-by-side in deep silence. Red Houston came eagerly loping up to them with his boyish face split wide in an engulfing grin.

“Folks want to know when they should circle, Mister Butler.”

Kit raised an arm and pointed to a meandering

creek that shone blood-red in the late sunlight. "Tell 'em when we get to that creek, Red."

The boy loped back down the south wing of the wagons. Lige laughed. "Wished I was his age again."

"Or had his feeling of adventure," Kit said, smiling. "Well, let's turn the leaders, Lige. They can circle when we hit the water."

The lead wagons were ready to turn inward by the time Kit and Lige got back to them. The word had spread rapidly, thanks to Red Houston. The two scouts sat their horses out a ways, clear of the dust and turmoil, until the men were double-tonguing the wagons to seal the circle, then they rode down, and into the enclosure, swung down, unsaddled, and turned their weary animals loose.

Lige went as far from the clustering people as he could and began to make a hole for a cooking fire. Reuben Burgess came up to Kit and faced him. There was a deep stratum of humor in the old man's face. It had nothing to do with what he said.

"Fires, Mister Butler?"

"Kit. Folks just call me Kit. Yeah, if you folks'll always remember to make your supper fires early and douse 'em when the darkness comes, you won't get potshot from beyond the circle."

He walked away from Burgess and sought out Reaves. The emigrant's face was rested-looking and Kit suspected that he had crawled into a wagon and slept away the afternoon. "Reaves, go among the men and pick out about fifty who can stay awake for six hours and post 'em beyond the circle about a quarter of a mile."

"Sure, Kit." Reaves turned away.

"Wait a minute. Tell them not to come back to the wagons even when their six-hour stint is up. Stay out there and I'll send out the relief. They can sleep right beside the men who come out to relieve 'em. Understand?"

"Sure."

Kit watched the women and girls making cooking fires. The smell was good and it got better when the scent of food arose. He saw Allie beckoning to him and went over. She was standing beside a shorter, plump woman, who she introduced as her mother. The older woman studied Kit's lean, tall frame and tired face with a close and inscrutable look, then she asked him to eat with them.

"Thanks, ma'am, but my pardner's making . . ."

"I'll get Lige," Allie said swiftly, with the same crafty look of amusement in her eyes that her father had worn. She moved away. He swung quickly and caught up with her. They walked among the throng of people side-by-side.

"What's so funny to everyone, Allie?"

"What do you mean?" She was looking at him with mock inquiry.

"You know cussed well what I mean. Lige came from eating at your wagon with a grin fit to bust.

A little while ago I talked to your paw and he was laughing at me, too. Now you . . . you look like you're pretty tickled, too."

"I'll tell you after we eat."

She wouldn't be drawn out, either, until after all five had eaten heartily. Then she smiled boldly to him across the fire, and he asked her if she'd like to walk a little with him. No one spoke at the fire until after they were gone, then Lige held the Burgesses attention with tales of the Indians. Lige was doing his clumsy best, as he had done at noon.

"All right, Allie. What's it all about?"

She stopped where fewer people were and where the horses and cattle were cropping the tall grass, and she burst into laughter. He had never seen her so amused, and stood by darkly, waiting for an explanation. "When you're ready, ma'am," he said stiffly.

"Lige is wonderful," she said with the laughter making her eyes shine. "If you knew Dad better, you'd appreciate it more."

"What's he got to do with it?"

"Well, you know how he feels about slavery. After his talk with you this afternoon, he wasn't thoroughly satisfied about your slavery leanings. When Lige came riding up, Dad asked him about you. That's what was so funny. Even Dad started to laugh after Lige had gone, and all of us have been convulsed all afternoon."

"What'd that dog-goned Lige say?" Kit asked uncomfortably.

"He told Dad you didn't own slaves, never had, and were dead set against slavery. Then he enlarged on it to the extent of telling Dad how you'd always helped down-trodden people, were a pillar of virtue, a wonderful person, and probably the only man he'd ever known who could scalp an Indian on a dead run without dismounting from your horse. That you could crawl into a teepee and crush a skull and crawl away again without arousing anyone, and that you'd make probably the best son-in-law on the whole frontier."

Kit groaned and ground his teeth together.

Allie was still laughing inwardly. "Oh, Kit, you've no idea how glamorous he made you. So wonderful at things that made my mother's hair stand straight up. But he did it with classical enthusiasm, never once thinking he might be horrifying his audience." She could see the anguish on his face and reached out a little and touched his sleeve. "I want you to promise me something, Kit."

He shook his head vehemently. "No."

"Yes. You must. After all, Kit, he was doing the best he could to help you in the way that seemed most plausible to him. You just can't say anything to him about it."

"Why can't I?" he demanded in anguish.

"Because he thinks he was a great help to you. Don't hurt his feelings, Kit."

"Dammit, how about *mine!*"

"And don't swear!"

"Excuse me."

"He actually did make Dad and Mother interested in you, and they think Lige is just wonderful. Especially Dad. He puts almost as much store on loyalty like Lige's as he does on anti-slavery."

Kit slumped a little, staring back up where the shadows were growing dense and little red flickers showed the dying cooking fires. "And I'll give you odds," he said disgustedly, "that the old devil's sitting up there right now, telling your folks how he's lifted the hair of a dozen Blackfeet or Snakes."

"I don't doubt it," Allie said softly, watching his profile. "It ought to show you something, Kit."

He turned and looked straight at her. "What?"

"That emigrants don't understand your kind any more than you understand them. You think they're fools and stupid and worse, and they think mountain men are savages, no better than Indians."

"We've *had* to live like the Indians, Allie."

She nodded gently. "I can see that, but the others can't. Not yet." She cocked her head a little at him. "Have you found that emigrant men can fight, yet?"

"Sure. We found that out right after Powers got killed."

"Right after you showed them what to do, you mean," she said. "Well, they've also come to discover that mountain men have reasons for being as hard and brutal as they are. It's the land . . . the environment, Kit. By the time we reach Fort Collins the emigrants, as you call them, will understand you and Lige, too."

"Maybe," he said. "It won't matter, Allie. *If* we reach Fort Collins, that'll be the end of the trek for Lige and me. You folks'll go on and maybe you'll tell your grandchildren about the savage white scouts you had on this passage. That's based on a big if."

"They didn't bother us this afternoon, Kit."

"Sure not," he said. "They've probably pulled out and gone up to the gap to get ready for us when we try to go through."

"We could send out men. . . ."

"We don't have enough, Allie. Listen, they could make up two war parties, put one in the gap, and have the other one just standing by, watching. That's what I think they're up to. If we go into the pass, they'll go up there and roll boulders down on us, shoot fire arrows, kill the animals, and bottle us up in there. After that it'd be murder." His eyes were dry and hot-looking.

"Or, they can put one war party up there and wait for me to guess that's what they're up to and lead men away from the wagons to chase them out of the pass. You see? After I'd ride out with the men, the other party'd slip in and overwhelm the wagon train. Pretty simple that way, isn't it?"

"Are they that clever?"

He made an annoyed sound and glowered at her. "They're every dog-goned bit as clever as we are. Because their hide's red doesn't mean they aren't plenty savvy, Allie. By now you ought to know that. You've seen their strategy enough."

She turned slowly and walked over where a great, gaunt outline became a Conestoga wagon. She leaned back against it. The late moon was up a little, stronger than it had been in a long time. It showed the deep blue shadows in her ebony hair and the lighter blue circles under her eyes.

He followed along morosely, reached up, and knuckled his hat back with a weary gesture. The horses watched them drowsily, full and contented-looking. Most of the cattle and oxen were lying down, chewing their cuds placidly.

"Then how are you going to get us through the pass, Kit?"

He looked back at her with a troubled glance. "How? I don't know. I've got an idea, but it's pretty cussed weak."

"What is it?"

He shrugged, lost in the exhausted maze of his mind, feeling dreary and dirty and drawn-out almost to the limits of his strength.

"Find another pass?"

"There isn't another one, Allie," he said. "North about two hundred miles there's Rapaho Gap. We'd have to go back the way we came in here, then cut smack dab across the heartland of Dakota country." He lifted his glance and held it on her liquid, gray eyes. "We'd draw every cussed hostile Dakota down on us within two days. It'd be suicide."

"It looks to me like we already have most of the savages in the West around us."

He laughed shortly, harshly. "That's only the men of war from two bands. The Dakotas are about the biggest, strongest tribe of Indians in the high country. They can put three or four thousand darned good warriors in the field in a matter of a couple of weeks. No, it may look bad to you, Allie, but it could be a heap worse."

"What's your plan, Kit?" She waited. When he didn't answer right away, she said: "I have a lot of faith in you. We all have."

"I wish you didn't have," he said brusquely. "Allie. . . ."

"Kit . . . I . . . tell me what you think we ought to do."

He stood motionlessly, looking at her. His jaw muscles rippled softly. For some reason she wouldn't let him get past arm's length. It angered him. "We ought to fly over the pass," he said, turning away, "or go back."

She watched him stride with his long, springing step back up toward the dying fires. She followed slowly, not once losing sight of his figure until he dropped down at her parents' fire beside Lige. She came up moments later and took her place, avoiding his eyes.

Lige sighed and let his conversation die. He looked up at his partner, seeing the deep resentment, the near anger in his blue glance, and dropped his head with a small, uneasy scowl.

Reuben Burgess poured coffee into a tin cup, dented and battered, and handed it to Kit. "What do you think our chances would be, Kit," he asked, "if we sent a strong party ahead to Fort Collins?"

"About the same as a snowball in hell," Kit answered bluntly.

Lige looked up, shocked. Burgess's eyes widened and Allie flushed with displeasure. Only Mrs. Burgess didn't appear to be horrified. "Why?" she asked, just as bluntly, almost challengingly.

"In the first place, ma'am," Kit said, "in order to get through, you'd have to send at least a hundred men. We don't have that many. In the second place, the Dakotas'll be watching every move we make from now on. Their last good chance lies at the pass. If we get past them there, they can still worry us, but their best chance to wipe us out is up ahead. In the third place, for all your men are learning, they'd make too much noise and wouldn't know how to get through."

"All right," Mrs. Burgess said matter-of-factly. "Is there a way out of this barrier we're up against? You certainly didn't lead us this far without thinking of some way to get beyond the pass."

Before Kit could answer, a gun exploded south of them with a startling smash of noise. Kit and Lige jumped up as if they were coiled springs. Men began to yell and hurry toward the sound.

Running, the scouts arrived ahead of the others. A tall, wild-eyed youth was standing beside a dead Indian. His face was as gray as dirty snow. Kit caught him by the arm as Lige lunged past heading for the wagon.

"What happened?"

"I dunno for sure. I was goin' to the wagon to fetch out my bedroll and I heard this owl cry. It sounded like it warn't more'n fifty feet from the wagon. Reckon I was sort of keyed-up, anyway. I was standin' there, lookin' out into the night when I heard this second owl call, right inside our danged wagon. I knew it was an Injun . . . hell, no owl'd be in there. I was goin' forward when I seen this buck come slippin' out over the tailgate. I shot him."

"Kit!"

He dropped the boy's arm and looked up. "What's in there, Lige?"

Lige dropped to the ground and walked over beside him. "They sure come close that time. Went and poured the coal oil out of a lantern all over everything." He nudged the limp Dakota with his foot.

"Must've been all set to fire her up when the lad here come along and the buck out in the grass called a warning."

People were standing with hanging jaws, looking from Lige and Kit to the dead Dakota. Kit kneeled and rolled the Indian over. The bullet had pierced his lungs, evidently at close range, too. Kit started to arise. The night was as still and tense as the people in front of him.

From just beyond the wagon circle a man called out in a terrible voice, in Dakota: "You will go no farther, white people. You will go no farther!"

The emigrant men surged forward. Kit threw out his arms. "Let him go. If you go out there, you might run into ten more of 'em."

"They're awful slippery," Lige said placatingly.

The men milled closer around the fallen warrior. The women were white-faced. Kit turned to the lad. "Go get a blanket or something to cover him up." He swung back and saw Red Houston, puffy-eyed as though he had been asleep. "Red, round up some of your crew and bury this feller."

He and Lige walked back through the moving emigrants. The lad who had shot the Indian caught up with them. "What about the wagon?"

he asked. "Hadn't a body best stay in there tonight?"

Kit shook his head. "No, just tell your folks to clean up the mess and get the oil-soaked stuff out of there." He started on. "Lige, I reckon that'll put 'em on their toes for a while."

"Yeah. You go roll in for a while, Kit. I'll see to the change of guard and what-not."

Chapter Eleven

Kit went down the wagons until he found their little camp with its half-finished fire hole, unrolled his buffalo robe, kicked off his boots and hat, and rolled up into it. He was asleep almost before he had closed his eyes.

Lige went among the people telling the men to get rested. He used the older boys as guards, too, stationing them under the wagons all around the circle. He didn't think there was much danger now, but after what had happened he knew the emigrants wouldn't feel like sleeping anyway, so he used them to double up on the guarding wherever he could, with the solitary exception of the fighting men. These he insisted get some sleep.

The night was balmy. A lot of people who had stolen snatches of rest during the day were huddling around the dead fires. Some wore coats and blankets around their shoulders. Others, younger, needed no covering beyond what they wore. At the Burgess fire Lige dropped wearily down. He could see the latent fear in their faces.

"Pretty close at that," he said quietly. "Cussed guards . . . well, they're slippery all right. I guess a man hadn't ought to blame 'em too hard, at that. I've had them slide past me in the night, not five feet away." He picked up a charred stick and poked aimlessly at the fire. "If they'd've fired that wagon, there'd've been the devil to pay for sure."

"What was it?" Burgess asked. "One of the young roosters?"

"Yeah. A hot-blood. There's always a few that'll risk being killed in the dark for a chance to count a big coup." Lige smiled tightly. "It'd've been quite a coup at that, if he'd brung it off."

"Do you think they might try it again," Mrs. Burgess asked, hugging a black shawl to her plump shoulders, "or others might come?"

"I doubt it," Lige said slowly, dropping the stick and looking fully at Allie as though his mind was on something else. "It'll show 'em we're awake. They'll take heed, I figure."

Allie saw Lige's stare and wondered about it. She shifted her position a little before she spoke. "Lige? Why won't Kit tell us what he's got in mind?"

"Well, I reckon, ma'am, because he hasn't got anything in mind. The boy's plumb wore to a frazzle. Don't know as I've ever seen him look so weary, and, by golly, I've seen him go a long time on less'n he's getting here, too."

"It's the weight of responsibility," Reuben Burgess said.

"Might be," Lige acknowledged, not fully understanding what the words meant. "Might be. I think it's just too danged many hours of fighting and no sleep, myself."

"He must have something in his mind, Lige," Allie said softly, watching the older man closely.

Lige shrugged. "Might at that, ma'am, but I don't think so. I know him pretty well, and if he did have some scheme a-cooking, he'd've told me, I think."

They fell into a long silence for a while, then Reuben Burgess spoke while combing his beard with hooked fingers. "Do you think there's a way to go through that gap?"

Lige looked into the fire before he answered. "I can't see it, if there is, I'll tell you that."

Allie said vehemently: "The way Kit explained it, we can't go back . . . so we'll just have to go ahead."

Lige looked at her lazily. "You got any ideas, Miss Allie?" he asked in a dry drawl.

She shook her head. "Couldn't we make peace with . . . ?"

"After killing around thirty of 'em? Not a chance in the world. Not a single chance in the whole cussed world, ma'am."

Allie's eyes widened. She stared at Lige without making a sound, then, very abruptly, she got up, dusted her skirt, and turned away.

"Where you going, honey?" Reuben called after her.

"I've got an idea, Dad. I'll be right back."

They watched her until the shadows swallowed her, then Lige lay low on one elbow and smiled softly, warmly. "She's got grit, that gal," he said. "He couldn't do no better anywhere, I don't think."

Reuben and his wife fixed unmoving glances on the old mountain man's face without Lige being aware of them at all. He was watching Allie disappear into the mellowness of the hushed encampment.

She threaded her way among sprawled men with their fingers curled numbly around guns, past the dry-eyed women and sleeping children, beyond the ragged little individual family units that were scattered among the trampled grass and over to where Kit lay. She stood gazing at him for a moment before she got a solid shock. His eyes were open and fixed on her with unmoving, unblinking intensity.

"I thought you'd be asleep."

He smiled and propped himself up on one arm, gazing up at her shadowed outline. "I have been. I reckon a man gets used to no more'n four or five hours of the stuff, after he's gotten no more for the last years."

She kneeled and put her hands in her lap. "Kit, I have a plan."

"Good . . . so have I . . . let's hear yours."

She studied his face with its stubble of rusty beard. "No, let's compare them," she said.

His smile widened. "All right. Shoot."

"We could send Lige ahead by himself. He knows the country and the Sioux. He could make it to Fort Collins and bring back help."

He let the smile fade slowly, looking at her. "You're not far off, Allie. Only thing is, Lige's more valuable here."

"What do you mean? Who else could . . . ?"

"Me." He straightened up and crossed his legs under him. "It's about like this. If we wait another day, we'll be too close to the pass and they'll be expecting us to send out someone to try and get past 'em. Tonight, alone, one man who knows his way in the country just might make it. By dawn he'd be far enough toward the gap so's they would have to have pretty flung out scouts to find him. Especially if he went north a long ways."

"Not you, Kit. We need you here."

He shook his head. "No, you don't. Lige's as good at this siege business as I am. Maybe better."

"But it won't be a siege, will it?"

"I think so," he said slowly. "Did you hear that buck holler out? The one beyond the wagons? Well, he said we wouldn't go any farther. That's the same as saying they've got us surrounded. Maybe he was bluffing. I sort of think he was, in a way. In another way I think some of the hot-bloods are out there."

"You mean we can't move, at dawn?"

"Sure, we can . . . but we won't, Allie. We've got

water here and good grass. We'll just do like the buck says. We'll stay right here. You all will, I mean. Stay right here and wait while I ride for the fort." He saw her interruption coming and waved it off.

"Allie, they're split up. Half waiting on the cliffs above the pass, half or less down here. That'll mean you'll only have half of 'em to fight for a day or two, until they figure out what's happened. It'll save you that much longer. If you go any closer to the pass, they'll jump you. Do you understand?"

"Yes," she said in a low voice, "but Kit . . . not you."

"It's got to be me."

"Can't Lige do it?"

"No. I mean . . . yes, he *could* do it . . . but I don't want him to. He's better here. Besides, if I'm caught, maybe I could talk my way out of . . . what they'd do. Lige couldn't."

"You couldn't, either," she said with rare insight, settling lower on the ground and looking strangely defeated.

He didn't argue with her about it. "Anyway, Allie, one or two might make it if they knew where to go and how to slip around them." He frowned suddenly. "And maybe there aren't any soldiers at Fort Collins, too . . . only don't tell anyone that. No sense in knocking folks' hopes out from under 'em."

"There must be, Kit," she said, looking up with widening eyes. "There's *got* to be!"

"This isn't the only part of Dakota country that's afire, Allie." He ran his hand through the blond thatch of his rumpled curly hair, and looked over where his horse stood, sleeping, filled and rested. As though thinking aloud, he spoke again. "If I pull his shoes, they might think it's just another warrior track. If I don't, they'll track me to hell and gone . . . but the horse'll get tender-footed crossing the rocks." He swung to face her with a rueful grin. "Sure's a heap of decisions to make, aren't there?"

"I'm afraid, Kit," she said in a small voice, her smoky-gray eyes like a winter dawn, in color.

"Me, too," he said, still grinning, feeling the fierce tug under his heart at the beauty of her, there in the soft, fragrant night. "I get scairt every time I get into a fix like this . . . and I get sick and tired of sitting around where there's no chances to take. Hell of a note, isn't it?"

"Don't swear."

"I forgot."

She let her gaze fall away from the hot, bold stare he wore, but not for long. The troubled depths of her eyes were writhing with foreboding. "No other way, Kit?"

"You know there isn't, Allie. You came over here with an idea like mine. If there was another way, we'd've thought of it. Going into that gap is plumb out, we all know that."

"Yes," she agreed, still in the small, strained voice.

He moved on his robe. She threw him a quick, frightened look. "No, Kit. Wait."

How it happened neither of them knew. One moment she was three feet from him, rising on her knees and holding out both arms as though to stop him. The next moment they were clinging closely to one another, the deep, stifled thunder of their hearts making a surging pattern of excitement that raced in their veins.

He dropped his head and found her mouth. It was warm and moist. He moved his lips on hers and she clung to him with half-closed fingers that scored deeply into his flesh, under his shirt.

When he pulled back and looked into her eyes, they were almost black with dilated pupils. The little pulse in the soft, golden V of her neck was throbbing without restraint, in an erratic, savage way.

"Don't go, Kit. Please don't go."

"You're not talking sense, Allie," he said softly. "You know you aren't."

"Then take me with you."

He smiled. "Wish I could," he said, hugging her convulsively until she felt pain with the breathlessness that was robbing her of all strength. Bruising pain.

"I'll be as quiet as an Indian."

He shook her gently and frowned. "I'll come back to you."

She closed her fingers tighter and the hurt flared outward along his nerves from them. He bent slowly, bringing her up a little. She sought his mouth with her own. There were startlingly long, black lashes low over her gray eyes. He felt shut out a little by them, then he kissed her again, and she winced from the stab of his beard stubble, but held him tighter than ever.

When he released her that time, their faces were close. She could see the savageness in his eyes, the deep circles tinged with blue tiredness, the deep scores where lines met and scrolled their way into his bronzed face. She thought that she had never seen a man so handsome in so rugged a way. A man with such strength, and force, carved deeply into his features. His tousled hair was glistening dully, softly, from the milky wash of the moon.

He released her and pushed himself upright, held out a hand, and hauled her up by it. They stood very close, unaware of the universe and everything in it, looking at each other.

"Allie, will you be sorry we did that?" Kit said, tugging his boots on.

"No, Kit, I'll never be sorry."

"Don't sound so glum."

"How else should I feel?" she said with a break

and an edge in her voice. "How would you feel if we were different? I mean . . ."

"I know what you mean, Allie. I'd feel about like you do, I reckon. Only it doesn't help any. I'm leaving you behind, too. I don't feel very good about that. They may make an all-out effort before I can get back."

"If you get back," she said fiercely. "Kit . . . Kit, take someone with you. Two would be better than one."

"No," he said, with a quick shake of his head. "Lige'd be better'n going alone. Besides him, there's no one here who could do it. You," he said, his little, old-looking grin tugging downward at the corners of his mouth, "you move softly. I've watched you walk, Allie. You'd make a top-notch scout."

"Then take me," she said in her quick, breathless way.

His smile widened. "Like I said before . . . wish I could . . . but that's plumb out." He looked up at the purple night with its widening sickle of a moon. "Well, Allie, I reckon I'd best go tell Lige and get moving." He groped for her hand and donned his hat. "Come on. We'll walk up there together."

Only Reuben Burgess and Lige were by the cold fire hole. They both watched them come up. Lige sat up with a lop-sided yawn.

Kit held Allie's hand until the girl was seated,

then he dropped down on crossed legs and told Lige what he had in mind. Burgess didn't say a word. He hardly breathed, in fact, and Lige didn't look much different, until Kit was finished. Then he sucked in a large chest full of air and exhaled it slowly, fished for his twist of tobacco, and held it in one grimy paw, staring at it.

"I thought of that, Kit. Thought of it while I was lying here. Fact is, I figured I'd be able to make it better'n you would."

"How, Lige?"

Lige bit off some tobacco and poked the twist back into a pocket. "Oh, just things," he said vaguely, looking at Allie's face from beneath shaggy brows surreptitiously.

"Like what?" Kit persisted.

Lige looked at him in annoyance. "Well, for one thing, if you want me to talk right out . . . I'm leaving no one behind."

Kit nodded quickly, understandingly. "Thanks, Lige," he said. "I figured it'd be something like that. But I think you're better here with these people. I might be able to get off if they catch me. You wouldn't. White-Shield-Owner and Big Eagle are . . ."

"Huh?" Lige grunted dourly. "Twice they tried to talk you out of it, boy. Now . . . no! They'll slit your hairline just like they would anyone else's. Remember, Kit, we've led these people against 'em more'n once. They know who figured out that horse-stealing trick. That was Indian strategy . . . not white man. They know, Kit. Your blamed hair'd look fine on a coup stick. Don't ever think you'll wiggle out, if they catch you, because you won't, and I think you know it."

"All right," Kit said brutally, getting up with a lowering thundercloud on his face. "But I'll chance it. Someone's got to, and I think I'm the one most likely to make it. Lige, keep the wagons right here in this circle." He talked fast, bluntly, watching Lige's head drop lower as the older man listened. The sound of his voice was almost the only sound; the hour was late.

When he had finished speaking, Reuben Burgess got up and held out his hand across the dead fire. "If prayers'll help," he said, "mine'll go with you, Kit."

"Thanks." Discomfited, he started to spin away. Allie was standing, facing him with a stricken look, like an illness, in her face. He groped for her hand with hot blood running inside him. "S'long, Allie. I'll come back." She held his hand but he pulled away and walked swiftly back down where the horses were.

The night was mute with a filtering of small, inconsequential sounds. Horses stamped their hoofs, men snored, and cattle grunted. His horse was gray with dried sweat salt. He found a swathing of grass that hadn't been foraged under a wagon, tugged it up into a switch, wet it at the creek, and went back to the horse and curried its back briskly. A sore back would be a hindrance, as much as tender hoofs.

He saddled and bridled the beast and led it to a place where two lanky boys, who had already pulled down the barricade, stood watching him with wide, wondering eyes, but saying nothing. He stopped and looked at them. Neither was the red-headed Houston boy. He smiled.

"Hold your fort, men," he said in a quiet way. "Out here you get to be men almost before you're boys. Hold your fort and keep 'em outside and you'll live to tell how it was done in the old days."

"Are you leavin' us, Mister Butler?"

"I'm going to Fort Collins and see if I can't fetch back some soldiers, boys. When I get back, I want to see you two still standing up, so remember what I tell you. Don't let a Dakota get inside your circle."

"We won't, Mister Butler." The smaller of the two, possibly a late seventeen, made a shaky smile. "Hope you . . . I bet you make it, too," he said. "It'll be risky, won't it?"

Kit nodded and toed into the stirrup. "Yep. It'll be risky, but if you'll do your share, I'll do my damnedest to do mine. Is that a good trade?" he asked, swinging lithely into the saddle and grinning down at them.

"Yes, sir! Good luck, Mister Butler."

"Good luck to you, too . . . men."

He wheeled and rode slowly, very cautiously, northward. He knew there were Dakotas out in the grass somewhere. If he had to shoot his gun, it would alert every Indian who heard the shot. They'd place the sound beyond the wagon circle and guess the rest.

His horse's ears plus his own trained vision were what he had to rely on. He used both, as well as an inherent caution and years of experience.

The grass made soft, whispering sounds, barely audible, as he rode through it. Far out, he reined up and looked back. The wagon circle looked a hazy white, like a monstrous glow worm curled into a sleeping circle. It was a ghostly specter from where he swung down finally, laid flat, and pressed his ear to the ground. He expected to hear nothing; it was simply an added precaution.

But he *did* hear something—a horse coming, and in a trot. He pressed hard, biting his under lip, concentrating on the direction of the sound. South. South and a little east. He stood up quickly, scowling with a black anger surging in him. Someone was coming from the direction of the wagon train, and by the time they got out as far as he was, it would be too late—too much of a delay to him—to send them back.

"Damn that Lige," he murmured.

He mounted swiftly and rode back in a fast walk, seeking the fool who had ridden out so recklessly, hoping to find him before the Dakotas who might be close sunk an arrow—as silent and deadly as the vaulted night itself—into his body.

The rider slowed his horse a little, as though precaution had come belatedly. Kit frowned. That wasn't like Lige. Maybe those boys back at the . . .

"Ki-itt!"

It came so softly, so gently and quietly, he wasn't sure he had heard it. Like a sigh on a little breeze, borne outward in an echo. He stopped and saw the outline. His heart sank.

"Allie!"

She rode up beside him and only slowed, but didn't stop. He had to turn and urge his horse to keep abreast of her.

"Allie, what in the devil . . . ?"

"Please, Kit. You said I could walk like an Indian." Her voice acquired a hardness to it he never heard her use before. "And . . . I'm not going back, so make your mind up to that. Anyhow, I don't think we ought to talk out here. Sounds carry." She turned her head and looked at him. As quickly as she'd flared out adamantly, she switched back to a soft, pleading tone. "Oh, Kit, don't be disagreeable."

Dumbfounded as he was, the need for speed was uppermost in his mind. Not horse speed, but a steady traveling until they got into the forest, then an even steadier hurry that might put them well above the farthest ranging Dakota scouts before dawn. He locked his jaws and stared straight ahead, afraid to say anything at all, feeling tricked and defeated and helpless all at the same time. He rode like that, holding his cold, angry silence until they were across the valley floor and rising toward where the first dark mass of forest showed a straggling fringe of new growth.

He swung in among the trees and left her to follow. His anger was fed by fear for her safety and the nagging knowledge of what might lie ahead for both of them. There were no trails, and in his bleak frame of mind he only glanced back occasionally. She was riding a good horse—thank God for that—and she was sticking to him like a leech. He grunted finally, and slumped in the saddle. Ahead was a swift-rising hill with tier after tier of tall black trees.

He traveled by instinct, like an Indian. Despite the detours he was compelled to make past giant, ghostly old deadfalls, he held to the northerly direction with unerring accuracy, but he made no move to rein up until he saw the skyline over the bony back of a humped-over mountain ridge.

Up there where the air was raw with pre-dawn chill, he stopped and looked back at her. She put a finger over her lips and smiled at him. In a way it struck him funny; in another way it exasperated him very much. He swung down and walked back beside her. She stopped her horse and gazed into his face with the reflection of starlight in her hair and gray eyes. Very gravely she kissed the finger over her mouth, leaned over, and touched the finger to his mouth.

He stared at her for perhaps a long, roiled minute, then shook his head like an annoyed bear, and sighed. "All right, Allie . . . dog-gone you . . . you win. But that was a tomfool thing to do. You know that, don't you?"

"Yes," she said in her small voice. Then she smiled and swung low from the saddle. "Kiss me, Kit. I was never so frightened in my life."

He kissed her, and felt the wild fire flame along the length of his body. "Oh, Lord," he said in a low, despairing whisper. "What can a man do?"

"Nothing . . . just get back on your horse and lead the way. I'll follow you."

He studied her in a puzzled way. "You told me, once, you didn't want anything to do with an Indian lover."

"No, I didn't. I told you I . . . well, what I meant was I wasn't sure *what* I thought of you."

"Harder to outguess than a Dakota," he said, still looking up at her.

"I *hope* I am," she said tartly in a low whisper. "You can think like an Indian too well. I'd hate to think you could outthink me, Kit."

"I've lived with Indians," he said gruffly. "That's how I got to know how they figure."

She flushed beet red. "Go get on your horse. It'll be dawn before long."

“All right. One more kiss.”

“No. You’ll get tired of them.”

He snorted softly. “Funny thing about that. The more of ’em a man gets the more of ’em he wants. Is it that way with women, too?”

“Yes.”

“Then bend down. . . .”

“No! Go get on your horse!” Her face looked scarlet and her eyes shone with a tawny, proud light.

“All right,” he said. “Later.”

They struck out along the high ridge, still heading north. She rode like his shadow with a triumphant shade of a smile on her face.

Chapter Twelve

He didn't stop until long after dawn, and by then they were swinging westward with the sun on their backs, heading down a hogback of land that rose gently within the forest. The ground was crested, flinty, and shallow, and only junipers grew. The land dropped away in a miles long gradual slope until it flattened out over a great plain. He reined up where they could see the vast plain for miles on end, tilting westerly with long shadows still on it. There were low-limbed junipers in a ragged way, to hide them as they sat there, looking.

"Don't see anything moving," he said softly.

"Are we past them, Kit?"

He shook his head. "Nope. We're just about parallel with the gap, Allie, but we're about fifteen miles north of it. This ridge runs through the forest to the pass."

"Fifteen miles," she said in a stronger voice, "is a long way."

"Seems that way," he said non-committally. "That plain down there, that's the one that leads to the fort. Makes you feel sort of naked, thinking about crossing it, doesn't it?"

She let her gaze roam over the bare expanse of land. There was something about all the openness that made her wince inwardly. An Indian could see two moving specks for miles out there. The forest at her back was like a friend.

"Isn't there some way around it, Kit?"

He lifted his reins. "Afraid not, Allie. If we followed the forest, we'd be going almost north. It'd be safer, maybe, to follow it for a few days, then drop south again, but it'd delay us three or four more days. They can't wait that long. Let's go."

He rode down the slope, utilizing all the cover he could, reluctant to ride out into the open to the very last. Wistfully he looked at a southerly line of scattered trees. They weren't on the way but they weren't too far off, either. The trouble was, there weren't more than half a mile of them, then prairie again.

She followed him out into the grass. He didn't glance back at her anymore. Her horse was strong and willing and, so far, so was she.

They hardly spoke all morning. A corroding tension was in them both. Several times he would twist in the saddle and stare for minutes at a time at the towering peaks that marked the pass, where he knew Indian sentinels would be.

They rode all day and stopped only once. That was when Allie untied a cloth bundle behind her saddle and offered him food. He was surprised at her thoughtfulness. They ate standing up, while their horses grazed, then pushed on. He watched her for signs of fatigue, but they didn't show until the following day, and then it might have been the late shadows of evening, but he knew it wasn't. She didn't ever say she was tired, though.

He wove his way among the little spit of trees they had seen from the hogback when they were leaving the forest. Finding a secluded spot he bedded her down, took his carbine, and squatted until late in the night, watching and listening. Once, he thought he heard horses. The sound never came again so, at dawn, they pushed on, leaving the trees behind.

The land didn't break until the fourth day, then it became a little uneven, as though warning the riders that rough country was ahead. Allie's food was dwindling. Kit just shrugged.

"Doesn't matter now, Allie. We can risk a shot if we have to."

"We're safe, aren't we?" She was watching his face.

He didn't look at her and his answer was slow in coming. "I reckon so," he said. "Ought to see Collins tomorrow." She knew he had switched the subject to cheer her, but didn't comment on it. It was hard, though, to keep from looking back.

Evening came gradually until the country finally lost its symmetrical sameness and turned into a series of serrated gullies and wrenched-up knobs that cast long, thin shadows. They were riding into the setting sun now, red and sulky-looking. He kept swinging his head, like a puzzled wolf. Turning it from side to side so his sun-pained eyes could watch the ambush country ahead.

They made their camp in a little dry wash near the pinnacle of a scrawny hillock. He made her lie down in his buffalo robe, took his carbine, and, toiling upward to the summit of the hill, squatted and froze, staring downward.

A soft contour, then another, then several, made his heart squeeze into a tight, hurting thing that quivered instead of beat. Unshod horse tracks and moccasin marks! An Indian had hunkered up there during the day, watching something. He looked out over the land. Nothing moved as far as he could see. The Indian could only have been watching one thing then—Allie and him.

With an oath he flattened against the ground and studied the breaks all around them. There were a dozen places Indians could be hiding. He strained to see which way the buck had ridden when he had left the knoll. Northward in an angling way.

He went down and saddled up with swift, fretting motions, shook Allie awake, and put a finger over her mouth. She got up as silently as a ghost, her eyes wide and dark with unconcealed terror. His expression told her enough. They mounted and rode due south, Kit in the lead, his carbine laying athwart his lap, his head up and his eyes on the fast-gathering darkness.

They were never sure when an erosion gully might erupt with riders, but they both clung to one thing. The darkness.

The night was deceivingly pleasant, warm, and refreshing. Then the moon came up. It was half full. Kit stared at it reproachfully. When they had needed night light, back at the wagons, they hadn't gotten it. Now they did.

He looked back once, shortly after midnight, and saw how Allie was sitting like a brittle stick, straight and tight with fear. Even with peril this close, he couldn't help but notice how statuesque, how handsome she was.

They labored up a long slope and stopped near the top. Kit left her holding the horses and crawled to the eminence, lay flat, and skylined the country roundabout for movement or silhouettes. There was nothing in front of them and it puzzled him greatly. Unless the Indian had been a Ute or Pawnee, or some other friendly, where had he gone with his knowledge that two whites were riding for the fort?

He got up and started back down the hill, frowning. When he was very close, he got the start of his life. An Indian was stalking Allie in the moonlight. He was still a long ways off, but he was slithering from shadow to shadow. Kit dropped low and raised his carbine. No, there would be others about. He gripped the gun by the barrel and scuttled like a rabbit for a little miserly clump of wiry sage that grew bleakly amid the short grass of the hillside.

The Indian, fortunately, was bent on counting coup. He was going to show his prowess by creeping right up within arm's reach of the girl. He would jump up and touch her with his hand—then shoot her. Kit could see the bow in his hand and the arrow held lightly by the same fingers. He couldn't make out whether he was a Dakota or not. It didn't matter.

Allie was standing with her weight on one foot. The horses, tired, were hang-dog, heads low. The girl was watching the country behind them with no inkling at all that death was coming for her on hands and knees, with muddy-black eyes and a thin, bloodless line for a mouth.

Kit moved only when the Indian did. He made his way deeper into the brush thicket, waiting. The buck would crawl that way to get close. The wait was murderous for the white man. The only person who showed no knowledge of the horror not fifty feet away was the victim. Kit's hands were clammy on the carbine barrel. He scarcely breathed at all when the warrior came stealthily close to the brush clump.

Then he swung the carbine like a club, and a second before it struck the Indian caught the wisp of movement and started to spring away. The gun butt missed his head but crashed with terrible force into his back, high up and between the shoulder blades. He crashed flat on the hillside and never moved.

Allie swung at the sound. Kit could see the hugeness of her eyes even at that distance. The moon paled her face to a sickly whitish-gray. The horses had their heads up, watching him get up on shaky legs, and bend over the Indian. Very deliberately he squatted by the buck, took the arrow from his hand, plucked out his knife, and made two long, deep grooves down each side of the arrow. He then pricked his finger and let the blood flow along one groove, held it a moment to set the blood, then turned the arrow over, and, with spittle and black earth, filled in the other groove.

After that he plunged the arrow deep into the dead Indian's body and strode down where Allie was standing, without a backward glance.

"*Hoppo*," he said shortly, and indicated what it meant by mounting his horse and reining southward. She followed.

The night kept its persistent ghostliness until he found another high ridge, but, thankfully, there were trees there again. He reined up and swung down, squatted, and stayed motionless for more than an hour. She stood beside him, holding their horses, saying nothing.

"There!"

He said it harshly, triumphantly, coming off his haunches with a smooth movement. He pointed his arm downward, along the drift of hillside where they had been an hour before.

"See 'em, Allie?"

"Yes." Her voice was leaden (which was how she felt), in spite of an effort to keep it from sounding that way. "They're Indians, aren't they?"

"Yeah."

The only way he had caught sight of them at first was because one of them had lit a pine-knot torch. It showed with a harsh brilliance against the dark bodies bending low over the dead Indian.

She looked at Kit's face. It was wreathed in a savage smile. It shocked her. As weathered and bronzed as he was and with the light so faint, he looked more Indian himself than he did white. "What are you smiling about, Kit?"

"They're scairt, Allie. Look at 'em. See how they're talking in sign language. It's too far and too dark, but I'll bet you they're for going back hell-bent-for-leather."

"What did you do?"

He grunted in a pleased way, watching the dim, distant outlines. "I marked an arrow with the signs of the Comanches. If there's one tribe the Dakotas don't like to tangle with it's the Comanches. Comanches only come this far north on war parties, and when they come, they kill everything they see that moves. That's what's making them hesitate now."

"Have they been following us?"

He nodded. "Yeah, since the day we came out into the open. I didn't know it, though, until I went back up on the hill when we stopped. It was good. They were making a surround. I can imagine why."

"Why?"

He shrugged, turning to their horses. "They know who it is who's making the run. Me. In Dakota they call me Ohiyesa. They want Ohiyesa alive to lecture to a little before they go to work on him. Thank God for that, Allie. Otherwise, they'd've just plain shot us both and lifted our hair to show the people back at the wagons. Let's go."

They went straight west after that and didn't slow up until dawn. By then Allie was over her fright and he had never seen how badly her body shook at all. They were riding down a valley when she rode up beside him.

"What does *hoppo* mean, Kit?"

"It's Dakota, Allie. Means . . . 'let's go'."

"And . . . Ohiyesa . . . your Indian name, what does that mean?"

"Means . . . 'The Winner' in English. I got it for winning a foot race one time, years back."

"It fits perfectly," she said.

He turned and made a wry smile at her. He felt greasy with dirt and exhaustion and drained-away energy. "I'll agree with you when we're back at the wagon train with a herd of yellow legs . . . soldiers."

Just before the sun rose, he was shaking his head sharply, from time to time. There was a fuzziness to his vision and a lethargic numbness stealing through his veins. She watched him for a while before she spoke.

"Kit, you've got to rest."

"Can't yet, Allie. Not this close to Fort Collins."

"Yes," she said, reining up. "Look, there's a bank of creek willows. Let's go in there." Without waiting, she turned her horse and made for the trees. He followed reluctantly, knowing he was very close to the end of his physical trail, but loathing himself, too, for giving out so close to safety.

"There," she said, swinging down. "Wash in that creek and lie over there where the moss is. I'll watch for them."

He stood, holding to his saddle horn with one hand. His legs felt like they were filled with fluid instead of bone and muscle. "Allie, I hate this. You don't know what to look for."

"Movement," she said. "It's daylight now. They won't get over that hill without my seeing them."

He went to the creek like a drugged man, dropped to his knees, and knuckled cold water into his eyes. It didn't help any. He washed hard, using fine sand for soap, then fell back on the moss and slept like a dead man.

The sun climbed higher. Twice he snored and she rolled him over. He didn't awaken until the shadows were creeping out from under the willows, spreading in an exploratory way, cautiously westward.

"Kit. Kit, honey. Let's go. *Hoppo*."

He awoke by opening his eyes and not moving a muscle. She was bending over him. Her jet-black hair was combed and looked too perfect for the disheveled appearance of her clothing. Brush had made a ragged hemline and had torn the little rents in the front of her dress.

She had scrubbed her face, it appeared. He sat up, looking around them slowly, letting his eyes study every brush clump and rock, every hill and tree.

"They haven't come, Kit."

"Then the arrow must've scairt 'em worse than I hoped it would. Good." He looked up into her face again. "You washed," he said.

"I took a bath," she said, rocking back on her haunches with a breathless smile.

"A bath?" He jumped up. "That's a bad thing to do right now."

"No, I watched. I took it in a place where I could see all around me."

He laughed. "It must've been a pretty picture."

She turned scarlet and stood up beside him. "The horses are rested, too. There's lots of feed under these trees."

He was looking at her in the same amused way. "Can I kiss you, now?"

She didn't answer him. She just went closer and reached up and put both cool hands on his face and melted against him.

"You need a shave."

He put both arms around her and held her to him without speaking or moving. She put her cool cheek against his face and the words tumbled like water from her.

"Kit . . . I've been afraid for so long . . . so long. I think I'm going to cry."

"We're almost there, Allie," he said in a low, soft tone. "Just a little longer."

"I want to wait," she said, "only I don't think I can." Her body shook and he tightened his grip a little. "And . . . Kit. You've aged so. You look thinner and older and tired. There're lines around your eyes." She drew in a big breath. "I won't cry, Kit. I won't cry."

He held her out a little and bent his face toward her with a gentleness he didn't know was in him. She came up on her toes quickly, almost fiercely, and kissed him. Her lips were hot and the long, black lashes were just a little damp-looking. His blood ran riot but he stood back and looked at her. The smoky film was in her eyes, a liquid softness, like gray clouds at evening.

"*Hoppo*, Allie."

"All right."

They followed the willow-lined creek for several miles, until it twisted in a tortured way, among broken gulches that seeped water into its main channel. Then Kit ran across an old buffalo trail worn smooth and deep, and followed it at an angle up a side hill and across the top and down the other side, where more little breaks in the land confronted them. He knew the way from there, too, and when at last they saw what looked like a mirage far ahead, they were heading in a beeline straight for it.

"Is that Fort Collins?"

"Sure is."

"It looks like a town, Kit."

He turned and looked at her profile. She had a tiny little frown on her face. He smiled. "What'd you expect, a regular log fort? Collins has been growing for some time now. It wasn't this big the last time I saw it, either, but you could tell it would be one day."

Chapter Thirteen

They rode the last five miles side-by-side. Reaction set in and Allie couldn't remember ever feeling quite as ill and weary as she did when they began to scuff trodden dust on the outskirts of the place.

Kit thought that Fort Collins had changed much more than he would have guessed it might. It wasn't altogether the new buildings, although there were plenty of those. Store fronts with the sap still oozing out of the green lumber and box-like homes were thrown at random over the landscape. Big garbage piles were heaped at the rear of the town and there were strong, springtime smells of sweaty horses.

It was more than that. There were people everywhere. The men in buckskin were a sprinkling now, a lost minority that belonged to a scene their blood made them a part of. In their hearts they still belonged to the country as it had been—Indian country.

There were respectable women, too. You could tell them by their drabness. Kit sighed, feeling nostalgia for the old Fort Collins. Allie shot him an inquiring glance. "End of the trail, Kit?"

"Yes," he said. He didn't try to explain what the sigh had really meant.

He took her to the Collins House, got her a room—no small feat in a town bursting with people and few facilities—and went to the Army post, after leaving their horses to be washed, rubbed, and grained.

He felt no different from the hundreds that swarmed just as dirty as he was, with for less cause, until he met the beak-nosed, hawk-eyed military commander. He was crisp in word and appearance. Clean with only the inevitable sifting of ingrained dust on him. And he listened with unblinking regard until Kit had finished his story, then he stood up and nodded once, very shortly.

"Where'll you be, Mister Butler, when we get assembled?" No question about how Kit felt, whether he could pilot them back, or anything else. Just: "Where'll you be when we get assembled?"

Kit liked the man and the way he acted. "At the Collins House, Captain."

"We can't plug the traffic in town. We'll meet you south of the last shack, in an hour. All right?"

The officer hardly waited. He was moving past Kit as he spoke. The hard, flinty eyes stayed on Kit's face with a barely hidden impatience and the thin mouth grew thinner. "All right," Kit agreed.

He was left standing in the little command hut alone. He turned stolidly, feeling as thick and oxen-like as he could in the face of this brisk activity, and walked back outside.

Allie had new clothes provided from some

generous and anonymous source when he knocked on her door and opened it. He stood in the doorway, looking at her. Her face was thinner, more mature, and longer-looking. It was as though he had left a girl, dirty and bedraggled, and had come back to face a woman. The sense of being gone a long time came over him.

"Do I look better?"

"Better? I never thought you could, Allie. But you do. You look . . . well, like a mature woman."

"Didn't I before?" She was watching him with a steady look.

"You looked like a scairt girl before." He closed the door and leaned on it. "You look older, too."

She laughed. "I never should have said that to you, Kit. I'm sorry, darling. But it hurt me to see you changing so."

He smiled. "Age doesn't mean as much to a man as it does to a woman, I don't think. We accept it more fatalistically. Women love youth."

"No," she said. "Not all women. I don't. I love you." It shocked him. It seemed almost indecent to say anything so bold and outright. He crossed to a chair and dropped down on it. She turned and put her hands behind her and leaned on the chifforobe, looking at him.

"You didn't want me to say that, did you, Kit?"

He nodded his head. "Allie, I reckon there're no secrets between us. I love you and you know it.

Have since the first time I saw you standing there with your arm across the black mare's neck." He smiled swiftly. "It takes time to get used to, though. Not me loving you, Allie. You loving me."

"Why is it any different one way than it is another, Kit?"

He dropped his gaze broodingly. "Well, for one thing I'm a scout. I've got nothing, Allie. Probably never will have."

"I don't care."

"You will, though, Allie, when the new wears off."

"No, I wouldn't, Kit. I really wouldn't. You don't know me well enough yet. I wouldn't care whether we never had anything more than the horses we rode and a big buffalo robe."

He believed her—and was awed. It was the truth. He could see it in her level gray eyes and strong face. A one-man woman, blindly loyal. A woman as loyal in her woman's way as Lige was in his man's way. He got up and crossed over to face her.

"Get a lot of rest, Allie. I've got to meet the Army south of town and lead 'em back."

She shook her head at him, took her hands from behind her, and ran them up his arms until they were on either side of his lean face. "We'll *both* go back, Kit."

"You're worn out, Allie. There won't be anything to going back anyway. I'll . . ."

"You're forgetting my mother and father are back there, darling."

He had forgotten it. He squinted at her. "I'll bet they're fit to be tied, wondering where you are."

She wagged his head gently back and forth with her palms, in a negative way. "They know."

"You mean they knew and didn't try to stop you?"

"They talked to me. You'll understand when you know them better, Kit. They've always treated me like I had a mind of my own. But they'll be worried just the same, if I don't come back with you." She pulled his head close and kissed him firmly on the mouth. "I have my own fear, too, Kit. I couldn't wait for you to come back and tell me if they're all still alive."

"No," he said. "I reckon not. But you haven't had much sleep, Allie."

"Hold me, Kit. Just hold me and don't talk for a minute. That's all the rest I need."

He swept her up and down with his bloodshot glance. "You look very pretty, Allie."

She leaned and he took her into his arms. A big, racking sob broke over her. Just that one, then no more, and she lay still and tall, against him.

"Allie, wait up here in the room until I fetch a couple of fresh horses from the livery barn. I'll signal you from the window. Then you come down and we'll go out to meet the Army."

"In just a minute," she said, stirring against him. "Just a minute longer."

He held her with the fullness of her like fire against him. Then he rocked her with a soft, instinctive movement. That was all it took. She started to cry. At first he felt a gentle pathos, but as the fury of the storm swept over her, wave after wave, he became uneasy and frightened and feeling helpless. When he would have pushed her away to ask, she clung the tighter. They stood like that for a long time, neither of them aware of the passage of time until a shattering blast of fisted knuckles rolled peremptorily across the door, making the room quiver and the chifforobe quake.

"Mister Butler? You in there?"

"Yes." He disentangled himself quickly, his face as red and guilty-looking as it could get.

"Captain Forrester sends his respects . . . and will you hurry. We're waiting."

"Be right there. As soon as I get horses. . . ."

"I have two downstairs now. Are you coming?"

"Two?"

"The captain said you had a lady with you."

"Oh," Kit said, frowning at the captain's perspicacity. "We'll be right down."

He turned back, but Allie was arranging her hair—of which not a strand was out of place—and her back was to him, her straight, long-muscled back.

"Ready, Allie?"

"Yes."

She swung and crossed to him in a flurry of fast steps. "Kit, I didn't know one human being could love another as much as I love you. It's painful and it's . . . almost indecent."

He smiled and reached up with a curled fist, tilted her head back so far he could see the little pulse in her throat, and kissed her with a hungry anguish. "I didn't, either," he said, "and I'd give anything to be able to take a year off and tell you about it."

"*Hoppo*!" she said, stepping away with her gray eyes like smoke on a windy day.

He laughed.

When they got downstairs the corporal was red-faced with impatience. He was stocky, with great sweat-stain crescents under his arms, and an unpleasant bleak cast to his jaw. He bowed low to Allie and led them through town in a reckless lope. Pedestrians jumped and cursed and Allie laughed at the teamsters' throttled, purple looks as they had to bite back their words when they saw her.

The soldiers were a sight she would never forget. There were two hundred and twenty of them. They had little guidons on long poles to designate their separate units and Kit rode up to Captain Forrester and introduced Allie. Forrester's testy, restless eyes became suddenly very still. She accepted the unvoiced compliment and rode a little closer to Kit.

They struck out in a shambling trot. The side-saddle bothered her and cramped the circulation in one leg, but she bore it, thinking of the way she had ridden in, like a man, astride, her billowing skirt an inconvenience and an annoyance that neither of them heeded.

The soldiers' horses were fresh and the men eager. Kit listened to Forrester. He had fought Indians from Mexico to Canada. He had a world of respect for them, and no love at all.

"They've just about stopped commerce out here, this past couple of years. A man might get used to the idea, Butler, if he knew when it would end, but there's no way of knowing. We think they're licked or pacified . . . and here they come, as wild as ever."

Kit had little to say until they got back on the big plains where the heat-hazed distance showed the twin peaks either side of the gap. Then he pointed toward it. "Beyond there a day's ride."

"Oh. That's Fargo Valley. The Indians have another name for it. The gap's what they call Place of Kills. I forget what they call the valley." Forrester looked at Kit with a narrow, hawkish stare. "They didn't go into the gap, did they?"

"No, we left them back a ways. No sense in getting where they'd dump boulders down."

"Of course not." Forrester hurried the troops and

rode leaning forward in his saddle. "Sometimes a horse is awfully slow, isn't it?"

"Depends on whether you're riding or running," Kit said. "I used to ride this country trapping. The spring up here was always beautiful."

"I never looked at it like that," the captain said. "How many did you say are in the wagon train?"

"Originally about a hundred and sixty, or so. They've lost several men and about thirty are wounded."

"What band of Indians is it . . . do you know?"

"Yes," Kit said. "White-Shield-Owner's band, and, later, some of Big Eagle's bunch."

"Huh! I had the Big Eagle bunch bottled up over on the Rosebud once. He's quite a battler."

Kit dropped back into his silence again.

When they stopped to rest the horses, Kit and Allie were surprised at the lack of weariness the soldiers showed. Allie commented on it while Captain Forrester munched dry rations and smiled. "They're tough. There're a few replacements, but mostly they're regulars. They're used to going three and four days on a handful of biscuits and a two-hour sleep rest." He looked over at Kit. "I've always thought that, in order to whip these Indians, you'd have to match them in everything, then go them one better."

Kit nodded, watching the men saunter around, ground grazing their horses. "That's right, Captain. That's what leaves so many dead emigrants out here. They think you can bring your manners and habits from the East and make this country like it. You can't. I told that to the people we're guiding. This is an altogether different land. You don't fight Nature here. You learn how to get along with her or you don't survive."

"You fight like the Indians fight, too, Butler. Don't forget that."

Kit brought his ranging glance back to the captain's face. "It isn't hard to do. White men learn to take scalps pretty darned quick."

They pushed on after nightfall, crossing the big grass prairie when the moonlight made the grass look like sheet silver. By morning they were almost back to the tree fringe. They had made much better time than Allie and Kit had made. Their horses were far better fed and rested and they made no detours. It was as though Captain Forrester was looking forward to a fight, trying to find Indians he could throw his troops against.

Kit wanted vengeance, too, but he felt uneasy about Allie. He rode off a little way to one side with her. They swung up into the trees and felt the humid, pine-scented shade almost instantly, and stopped to blow the horses when they had breasted the first spiny ridge. Kit helped Allie down. Her face was flushed and her eyes had a writhing anxiety in their depths.

"It's hard to wait, Kit."

He nodded, looking past her where the depth of

dark forest lay. "It won't be much longer now."

"I've been trying to hear . . . to listen . . . but . . ."

"We're too far for that. Another couple of hours, though, and we'll begin to slope down toward the valley floor."

"I wish we could hurry."

He regarded her thoughtfully. It was the first time he had seen her when her nerves were crawling like worms. Even when the coup-counting Indian had stalked her, she hadn't looked so badly shaken as she was now. He leaned against a tall old pine and half dreaded what they might find down in the valley. He, too, had been straining to hear sounds and had heard none. What made him more apprehensive than anything was the absence of Dakotas.

He knew they had sentinels high above the pass. He knew, too, that the dust stirred up by the Army's passage would be visible for miles, as still and crystal-clear as the summer daylight was.

"Butler!"

He shoved off the tree and watched Captain Forrester striding toward them. Allie was like a ramrod, straight and tensed.

"Butler, there's a scouting party coming up from the valley south of us."

"South?"

"Yes. They're riding west, as though they have been down the valley." Forrester's eyes were fixed on Kit's face.

If the Dakotas were scouting up this way, it meant they had received signals from a sentinel who had seen the cavalry before they got into the forest, or who had seen their dust after daylight, but hadn't seen the troops. He thought it likely it was the latter. Otherwise, the men of war wouldn't come in a scouting party; they would come in force.

"Are they mounted?"

"Yes."

His heart sank. There had been at least twenty who had retrieved their horses. It was also possible . . .

"Take me where I can see them."

He knew Allie was following by the sounds her skirt made when it snagged on little trees, but he didn't look around at her. The soldiers were standing perfectly still. They had heard enough to suspect what was up, and were waiting like statues. It made Kit's spirit rise a little, knowing they were the kind of men they were.

Captain Forrester twisted and turned until he was on a little wind-swept outcropping of rock where the ground was too shallow to support vegetation. There, a grizzled sergeant was squatting, head twisted, watching something off on their right and down in the valley.

Kit saw them instantly. Forrester kneeled beside him, saying nothing. The Indians were riding in a fast walk. Their horses looked tired and the riders seemed loath to urge them in the cruel heat that was filling the valley right then.

"What do you think?"

Kit ignored the question and continued to watch the Indians. They were a part of the Dakotas who had gotten their horses back. He was sure of that for several reasons. That meant, possibly, that the wagon train was still resisting.

"They're heading for the high country."

He got up when the Indians had passed from view and dusted off his knees. "Yeah. They've got a signal that something's crossed the plain. I don't think the sentinel knows it's an army, though. Not the way they're riding. If they knew how many soldiers were in the forest, they'd send men like the wind, to warn the others."

"Then the others must be down where the wagons are."

"Must be," Kit said, turning to Allie. "So they're probably still fighting, down there."

"Or plundering," the sergeant said dryly, getting up. Then he saw Allie and his mouth fell open. However, it was too late to withdraw it.

Kit bristled for a second, then he took her arm and piloted her back where their horses were and spoke over his shoulder to Captain Forrester. "Let's get moving."

Chapter Fourteen

They moved carefully after that, and Forrester finally asked Kit to guide them. He reluctantly left Allie's side and led the strung-out force among the trees until they came to a thinning of the natural cover, and there he reined up and beckoned Forrester over.

"Listen."

They cocked their heads. Distantly there came a tiny popping sound. Kit smiled and swung far back to seek Allie. She had heard. He could see it in her face. Forrester lifted his reins. "They're still alive. Let's go." He was starting to nudge his horse when Kit restrained him.

"Hold on a minute."

Forrester stopped and looked over at him inquiringly.

"The way the wagon train's placed, Captain, and the number of men you have, I think you can catch those Dakotas without having them slip into the trees where you das'n't chase 'em."

"Are they out in the open on all four sides?"

"Yeah. Only they've got the trees on the south side to run for. The thing is, they're afoot. We stampeded their horses. You can't circle around and get across the valley because their sentinels will see you and flash the warning, but you can hit the valley in a dead run and make a big surround, and cut them off on the south side as well as over here."

"How many are there up there, would you guess?"

"Maybe a hundred and fifty . . . maybe a few more or a few less."

"No more than a hundred and seventy-five?"

"No," Kit said. "I'm sure of that. They've lost some and they never totaled two hundred any-way . . . unless they've got some help since we've been away."

Forrester turned and jerked his head to the hard-bitten sergeant who served as his scout. "Ride about a mile ahead of us, Mike. When you can see the wagon train, get a pretty close count on the Indians. Hurry up. We'll be waiting."

The sergeant rode on by without a sound. Kit watched him go, then Forrester was speaking again. "If they're afoot, we stand the best chance I've ever run across of making them surrender. That'd be the best thing that ever happened out here. Be a hell of a blow to Indian pride and morale."

Kit watched Allie ride up and spoke before she could. "We're waiting for a scout, Allie. Just a little while longer." He saw Forrester's ques-tioning glance. "Her father and mother are down there."

"Oh." Forrester shot the girl a quick look, then

drew his reins through one hand with the fingers of the other hand. It was an old story to him, but he didn't like it any better now than he had the first time he had seen an escapee looking at the remains of the mutilated dead. There was a better-than-even chance here, though.

He looked up impatiently and Kit dismounted, picked up a pine twig, smoothed away the needles, and drew a dust sketch. "This is the train. This is the shape of the valley where it is. These are the trees south of 'em. The Dakotas'll be around here." He looked up at the captain. "You understand?"

Forrester nodded, then he turned and beckoned to three soldiers who were watching him from a respectful distance. "Come up here a minute, boys. There . . . see that map? Well, we're going to come down out of the trees about there." Kit drew a crooked line with his twig. "As soon as we're in the open, you split the men up. Half will go south . . . ride like the devil too, so you can be sure to cut the hostiles off from retreat into the forest. The rest of us will complete the surround."

"One thing," Kit said quietly. "They are fighting down there. Don't let yourselves be killed by the emigrants. Stay back far enough to be out of gun range."

"That's right," Forrester agreed. "And watch me for signals. If the hostiles give up . . . fine. If they don't . . . slaughter 'em."

Kit snapped the twig and got up with a granite look. He turned toward his horse and raised his glance just before he stepped up. Allie was looking at him. Their eyes met and held. He knew what she was thinking and broke the spell when he sprang up and settled into the saddle.

The red-faced sergeant came back. His shirt was black with sweat and his eyes shone like blue glass. "I'd call 'em maybe a hundred and fifty strong, Captain."

"What are they doing?"

"Looks like a siege, only I don't see but maybe six, maybe eight riders. Rest of 'em's afoot, crawling around in the grass. If we could find their horse herd . . ."

"That's already been done. The emigrants stampeded them."

"Oh," the sergeant said, then he cleared his throat. "Sir, they're Dakotas, all right. And it looks like the wagon train's about done, too."

Kit's blood chilled. "What do you mean?"

The ice-chip eyes swung a little. "They ain't doing much firing from inside the circle. About four-to-one, I'd say. One emigrant firing for about every four hostiles that fire. Low rate of fire power."

Kit lifted his reins and flung a hot glance at Captain Forrester. "Let's go."

The men mounted to the accompaniment of moving horses. There was a rustling, sometimes sharply made, where riders brushed against or rode over wiry little pines and firs. Kit looked around anxiously at Allie, then he leaned a little toward Captain Forrester.

"Can you detail some men to guard her?"

"Sure. We could leave her up here."

Kit shook his head quickly. "No. If they break through us, they'll make for the forest like wolves. She'll have to go along, but if you could put four or five men around her and sort of tell them to keep her back out of range, it'd be best."

Forrester beckoned up a downy-faced lad not over eighteen. "Corporal, detail yourself and four men to look after the young lady. Keep her clear of danger and don't let anything happen to her. Understand?"

"Yes, sir."

They were riding swiftly downward now. The little sounds of gunfire came more persistently. Interspersed among them was an occasional shout, high and distant, like the scream of a hawk in the pale, burnished sky overhead.

The trees began to thicken again when they were past the shallow, flinty hardpan earth. Kit urged his horse ahead of the captain in impatience. He wound among the trees like a snake. The cavalry horse was good at it, as though he had had much experience doing it.

When the last belt of trees grew thin, Kit was urging his horse into a shambling trot. The animal ducked and bobbed and suddenly another horse broke over into a clearing made by a deadfall, and Kit looked around. It was Allie, her skirt streaming and her face pale.

"Kit, let me go with you."

"No," he said sharply. "There's a guard detail to ride with you. Honey, don't get close to where the shooting will be."

She saw the excitement, the roiled fierceness in his expression, and knew it was useless to plead. She reined up her horse and a wave of sweat-darkened blue shirts swung around her. He caught a last glimpse of her scowling darkly at a worried-looking young corporal who had swooped down from behind with a squad of men and surrounded her.

Forrester called out. He reined up scant feet from the clear slope that emptied down into the valley. The captain clanked up and Kit noticed he had a big Dragoon pistol in his right hand. The brass ring in the butt of the weapon—for a lanyard—made an unnecessarily loud noise of a sudden.

"Butler, you stay with me. I want someone handy who knows the lay of the land so I'll be able to signal."

Kit nodded and swung his horse out into the open beside the officer. The troopers erupted from the shadowy covert like blue pebbles catapulted by an unseen hand.

Kit swung for a look behind them as they all broke out upon the valley floor. The mounted Indians they had seen from the ridge were specks against the sun-splashed distance. For a long moment they seemed to continue their way toward the gap, then, as Kit watched, they stopped. He grinned wolfishly. If they rode back as fast as they could, they'd still be cut off from their companions.

He twisted forward and had to slit his eyes against the unaccustomed smash of the dazzling sunshine. Up ahead, possibly two miles, was the shimmering outline of the wagon circle. There was a gray haziness hanging over it. His heart beat wildly. Lige would be lying under a wagon up there with fear like a solid ball of gristle under his heart. He had seen Lige like that before. The more frightened and desperate he became, the more adamant and forbidding his face got until it was set in a stony look of unconquerable defiance. He would be looking like that now.

Forrester waved his pistol-bearing hand, arm's length, overhead. The soldiers began to fan out across the long, narrow valley. Several of them raised the yell. Kit smiled inwardly in a harsh, bleak way. These were the regulars; the best fighting soldiers on the frontier. They were worth ten soldiers with unfaded, bright new uniforms. They were, in fact, the only fighting white men on the frontier, aside from the old scouts and mountain men, who were a match, man for man, with the mighty and terrible Dakotas.

Someone sang out a rolling, sing-song order. Kit looked to his right, where the cry had come from. The soldiers on that side began to swing inward a little, like a giant hook with the pointed end bent so as to cut off the Dakotas' retreat toward the forest.

He rode with the hot wind streaming past, jetting the water out of the corners of his eyes, looking for Allie and the little knot of men who would be guarding her. They were far back, loping their horses to keep a good distance, not too close. He thought she was looking at him and threw up an arm. Instantly she waved back. Then Forrester was shouting something. Kit couldn't make it out, but he hurriedly looked forward again.

They had been seen.

The Dakotas were jumping up out of the grass as if they were being jerked with strong ropes. He threw back his head and let off the keening scream of a fighting cougar. The soldiers nearest to him looked with jerky, bulging eyes at him. He was smiling when he reached for his handgun, palmed it, and cried out again. That time the sound carried and the Dakotas recognized it. They answered back with their own war cries until the troopers took it up and the day was ridged and tortured with ululating howls.

A little ahead of the charging, strung-out, thin

rank of soldiers were two guidon bearers. The little pennants whipped and sawed crazily. They looked out of place except for the ten-inch long steel lance tips that glistened cruelly above them as the bearers set their lances and lowered them like Dakota lance bearers.

Forrester roared in a powerful voice into the bedlam that was increasing. Others heard and understood and passed his order down the line until a distant officer flagged back understanding. Then the racing line south, scudding across the open country between the forest and the wagon train, bent still farther inward, like a fish hook, and until that extra spurt of speed showed the soldier strategy, the Indians didn't understand what was happening. When they did, finally, a great, trembling howl went up.

Kit watched them break and race wildly to get across the closing gap before the soldiers did. It was a futile, almost pathetic race, men against horses. The culmination was brought to a vivid climax when the troopers were close enough to shoot.

The sounds were small and telescoped by distance, but Kit could see the wreaths of dirty smoke and the speeding bodies go end over end in violent convulsions. Then the fish hook was completed and only Kit's upper wing of the line remained out of range. His, and the curving center.

By then, as though reminded of something temporarily forgotten, the Dakotas left off screaming and running, and threw themselves down in the grass, or kneeled, and opened up on the troopers with a scattering, uneven volley of gunfire.

Forrester cried out an order that was lost in a smashing fusillade. Kit could see him cursing, but he couldn't hear a word, then the officer was waving his arm again, signaling. Almost immediately the blue line was riding in an eye-stinging, dirty gray fog of black powder smoke. Kit cursed then, too. He couldn't see anything ahead of him to shoot at.

He stood in his stirrups, straining, unmindful of the soldiers until he heard Forrester's roar again, then he turned and found himself riding far in advance of the line. Forrester had drawn his men back and was flashing signals for them to complete the encircling maneuver.

An Indian leaped up out of the grass and called out derisively to Kit. He let off an arrow that rose and fell, then whirred past Kit's head. His horse was swinging low, turning, when Kit fired back. He missed, too. The Indian made an obscene gesture that Kit returned with one of contempt, then he trotted his horse back to the soldiers, whose initial charge had been completed. Though both sides were beyond accurate firing range, they were within bullet-carrying distance all right, so that they dueled back and forth without damage, while Forrester reined up and leaned over to spit dust, clear his throat, and turn to Kit with a calm and sweating countenance.

"The damned fools didn't even run for it, Butler."

Kit shrugged. "They knew they couldn't make it, Captain."

"Your friends in the train seem pretty tickled."

Kit turned his horse and hauled him up. The animal's breathing rocked him with quick contractions of its lungs.

The emigrants were standing up and waving sheets, blankets, clothing—anything handy. Their yells were faint and hoarse and Kit tried to figure which one was Lige. He couldn't, for the simple reason that Lige was lying under a wagon with his head down between his arms and his old rifle slanted downward, the barrel's end in the stained and beaten dust. He didn't move.

"Who's that big black devil there with no shirt on? The one walking around among the bucks? You know him?"

Kit looked and answered softly. "You ought to. You said you had him bottled up on the Rosebud one time."

"Big Eagle? I'll be damned." Forrester sat motionlessly watching Big Eagle strolling as scornfully as though he were perfectly safe among the men of war.

"You will be if he gets his hands on you," Kit said dryly. "They've quit shooting."

Forrester threw up his arm and wigwagged. Gradually the gunfire stopped. He turned to Kit with an ugly smile. "Now what? Make council?"

"Up to them," Kit said, relaxing, watching, and waiting.

Chapter Fifteen

The strange silence lasted for a long two minutes. Kit was straining to identify White-Shield-Owner among the Dakotas. He couldn't find him, but Big Eagle had completed his long stroll among the fighting men and had come back to the middle of the line.

Abruptly, a fully painted and richly garbed warrior leaped up with a terrific scream. Every eye, Indian and white, was fixed on him. Captain Forrester said something, but it was lost in the frenzied dancing the strange warrior broke into, punctuated by wild cries.

"*Hayoka*," Kit said.

Forrester was watching the savage with a puzzled look. He reined over closer beside Kit and bent his beetling, puzzled stare upon the Indians. They were becoming more and more excited as the dancer convoluted.

"What in the devil is wrong with him, Butler?"

Kit didn't answer right away. He twisted and looked backward. Far behind the line of soldiers was the bunched-up party of mounted Dakotas. They were craning toward their comrades, cut off from them by over two hundred stationary soldiers in blue with wide, yellow stripes down their dragoon britches.

He swept the landscape for sign of Allie and found her south of the main line and back a few hundred yards, her escort warily watching both front and rear.

"Butler! Dammit! What's the crazy fool doing?"

Kit turned and looked at the warriors again. The frantic dancer was moving backward, not forward, as he danced. He mimicked a warrior firing his arrows. Every dance step, every motion was a series of contrary movements.

Kit looked up and down the line and reassured himself that the troopers were alert, then he leaned toward the perspiring officer and spoke.

"That's a *hayoka*, Captain. In our language we'd call it Thunder Dreamer. They're very sacred."

"What a hell of a time to dance," Forrester said impatiently.

"No," Kit disagreed with a wag of his head. "When he's through dancing, they're going to charge us."

Forrester's head swung rapidly. "Are you sure?"

Kit inclined his head toward the *hayoka*. "Look for yourself. They do everything backward in their ceremonials. That one's imitating a man of war. He's showing that his power is great and his prophecy good. He's telling them they've got to breach your lines . . . that's what the running backward means . . . fighting past you and running for the trees."

Forrester looked angrily back at the dancing

Indian, then he swung his head up and down the line. Before he spoke, though, Kit interrupted his thoughts.

"Those mounted bucks are behind us. You'd better detail some men to watch them. As soon as the fight starts, they'll try to rake your rear."

Forrester called up an officer and told him how to neutralize the mounted Indians, then he swung back toward Kit. His face was beet-red and his eyes shone darkly. "I've been around them a lot, Butler, but I never saw one of those chaps before."

"I don't reckon you have," Kit said, without looking away from the dancer. "You've got to live with 'em to see *hayoka* ceremonials."

He grunted and jutted his chin.

"It'll be over in a few minutes. He's running down, getting tired. When it's over, they'll charge you."

"We won't wait," Forrester said, wheeling his horse and loping down the line.

Kit watched him spit out orders, then ride in a fast gallop up the northern perimeter of his huge half circle.

He worried about Allie and rode through the soldiers to where she was.

The young-looking corporal greeted him with an uncertain smile and a significant nod toward the distant mounted Dakotas. "We're liable to be between hell and high water, Mister Butler."

"You will be," Kit said, "if Forrester's detail

doesn't turn those riders back. Or at least hold 'em where they are."

"Oh. He's sending a detachment to take them out. We didn't know that."

"Watch them just the same. That's where most of your danger is. The bucks down in front will try to fight through the circle. I don't think they'll make it entirely, but a few may. Your job is here, not fighting Dakotas. If some get past, let 'em go, and stay well out of range of 'em."

Allie spurred up where he was talking with the corporal. Her glowing gray eyes had a penetrating clarity to them. He had an idea that imminent action did that to her, as it did to a man, making her see things twice as clearly as she would ordinarily see them.

"Kit, are they going to fight? Can't you talk to them . . . ?"

A great roar went up, and Kit turned his head swiftly. The Dakotas were bounding up out of the grass like grasshoppers. They were charging straight at the troopers. He looked for Forrester and saw him, his hat gone and his right arm wig-wagging fiercely. The troopers, with a thunderous cry of their own, threw their horses into a headlong plunge toward the dismounted Indians.

He had to fight down a macabre fascination long enough to look back at the mounted men of war. A streamer of blue-clad dragoons were whipping out in a much smaller semicircle from the original line, penning them in. The Indians were milling excitedly, as though willing to take on the troopers but lacking any decisive leadership. That was what Kit had been watching for. Now he was certain. He touched the corporal's arm.

"Watch her, pardner. When it's all over, stay with the soldiers, either way. If they retreat or go to the wagons, you stay right in among 'em."

"Kit!" Allie's voice was deep and frightened.

He put the horse down into a flat, ear-back run, and raced forward where the two forces had come together with a shattering suddenness. The confusion was indescribable. The men of war had an advantage only when they could get close enough to a mounted soldier to dodge the footwork of his horse. The fight broke up into a series of furious mêlées and the dust churned up into a high yellow cloud.

Indian death chants were everywhere. The *hayoka* had worked the warriors into a do-or-die fanaticism. They fought more ferociously than Kit had ever seen them fight. Once he caught a glimpse of Forrester, then the captain was gone in a whirl of dust and noise. Twice Kit saw Big Eagle. The stalwart buck, deep chest and coppery arms shiny with sweat and his face set in a craggy glare, fought with his legs wide. He, like almost any Dakota warrior, could keep half a dozen arrows in the air at the same time.

The riders held their advantage when they could chase or approach an Indian. In close, their animals were all but unmanageable with fear and a crow-hopping urge to bolt. Several Indians had managed to dislodge riders and were now mounted. One of these rode at Kit with a soldier's carbine held lightly in one powerful hand. Kit ducked and fired twice. The Indian rolled off the horse on the second shot, and Kit's horse paced his gait to miss stepping on the body.

The farthest section of the line held fast in spite of repeated assaults by Dakotas who were determined to break through and get to the trees beyond. Kit saw this dimly, through the stinging smudge of powder smoke. There was an officer down there who sensed the importance of keeping his line intact. He held it that way in spite of the smashing attacks by increasing Dakota strength and despite the battered, dented, broken line up where Kit was.

Somewhere, a long way off, as though from the sky itself, Kit heard the ripple of a bugle call. It surprised him for a second, in the heat of battle, then he turned to watch the soldiers. As furiously as they had accepted the Dakota charge, they were now drawing off. Kit's anger swam with a reddish froth before his eyes. If the soldiers retreated now, the Indians would take heart and renew their blind charge. They would break through.

He rode his horse up the field searching for

Captain Forrester. He didn't find him, and the bugle call came again. With the Indians' shouts taking on a wildly exultant sound, he raced back to the bugler, found him surrounded by Forrester and five non-commissioned officers, and slid his horse with reckless fury the last ten feet.

"Forrester! You can't pull 'em out now! The Indians're almost licked."

"We've got to re-group!" Forrester yelled at him. "The line's broken and the men're getting too scattered!"

"Scattered, hell!" Kit said furiously. He pointed where the steadfast fish hook was holding its ground against increasing Indian pressure. "That's the way to do it, Forrester." Apparently the bugle call hadn't been heard down there. He swung past the commanding officer and grabbed the trumpet from the bugler with a violent gesture. Captain Forrester turned on him with a set and deadly look.

"You fool! I know what I'm doing!"

Kit threw the bugle down. The bugler immediately dismounted to retrieve it. He was bent far over when a long Dakota arrow caught him under the right arm, pierced his chest, and knocked him sideways. Forrester was horrified. His wrath turned sickly at the sight of the dying man. Kit leaped off his horse and snatched up the bugle and turned toward several soldiers who were watching.

"Who can blow this thing?"

For a moment no one tried to yell back an answer over the bedlam, then a one-eyed, grizzled soldier held out his hand without speaking. Kit handed him the instrument.

"Blow the charge, dammit!"

The lilting call rang out with a mighty blast. The one-eyed soldier blew it again, as loudly and imperatively as before. He handed the trumpet back to Kit without looking at the officers, lifted his reins, and spurred his horse down where the line was wheeling, starting back with a roaring bedlam that was vengeance and eagerness, toward the startled Indians.

Kit threw the bugle down and sprang back into the saddle. He shot one triumphant glare at Captain Forrester and raked his mount mercilessly with his spurs.

Chapter Sixteen

The Indians had become badly spread out in the pursuit of the retreating soldiers. Now, afoot, they had no time to run back where Big Eagle was rallying a nucleus to stop the oncoming troopers.

Kit knew what the soldiers didn't know; that the Dakotas were all but whipped at the moment the retreat was sounded. He knew nothing of military science and therefore was unaware of the danger of having the soldiers broken up as they had been, fighting little individual battles with great gaps in their lines. His ignorance and Forrester's prudence, however, turned the tide completely, because, as the soldiers fell back to rally around the officers, they automatically closed up their ranks again, eliminating the gaps.

Now they swung and thundered back, a solid wall of blue, and the Dakotas, strung out, almost spent, reeled with surprise at this new maneuver—this new and violent charge—when they had been sure the soldiers were fleeing.

Kit and the one-eyed veteran were neck and neck for the lead when the blue column, like a quivering snake, struck the Indians again. Riding through and over them, they turned and flung out an ear-splitting roar of triumph as they raced back.

Kit saw Big Eagle standing as before. He could

see the war leader's lips move and his eyes glisten, but Big Eagle's death chant was lost in the pandemonium.

The bugle was sounding retreat again. Kit swore as the troopers veered off, firing salvos into the din and dust and gunsmoke, riding back as hard as they had ridden forward. Not until he was following them, flushed and feverish with the shock of battle, did he realize that Forrester could have him arrested.

He reloaded at the gallop and reined down to a walk when the firing died away to intermittent, popping sounds, down where the inward curve of the line yet stood fast, again despite the insistent call of the bugler.

Captain Forrester was rigid. His face was black as night and a big vein in the side of his neck throbbed. When he spoke, though, his voice was so low and deep Kit had to turn his head a little to hear him.

"You complete damned fool!"

Kit holstered the reloaded pistol and, resting both hands on the saddle horn, stared at the officer. Reaction, like a drug, set in. He had trouble finding the words he wanted. "It had to be done that way. They were scattered to hell and back. If you pulled out, they'd get clear. You know that."

"I also know that you can't fight an army in scattered parties, like you'd fight a mob.

Individually the troopers were at a disadvantage as soon as the bucks got past them and in close enough to grab a rider's leg. A solid front is the only way to fight a mounted line, Butler."

"That's the way they fought, the second time," Kit said. Forrester's savage glare was broken when a soldier trotted up to them and saluted the captain.

"He's dead, sir."

Kit looked around. Forrester returned the salute and nodded his head once, curtly. The trooper spun and rode down the forming line where men were dismounting and examining horses.

"The trooper who bugled for you, Butler, is dead."

"I'm sorry," Kit said.

Forrester didn't speak for a moment. "He'd be sorry, too," he said bleakly, finally, "if he'd lived. You shoot men for mutiny in combat."

Kit didn't respond right away. He was watching the wounded. Most were ambulatory. They were all congregating in one place where aid men were setting up an impromptu station for their care. The troopers were talking. Their voices floated up to Kit in a tinny, unnatural way. He looked out at the Indians and beyond, where the wagon train was obscured by the drifting dust and gunsmoke.

Kit made a tired gesture with one hand. "I shouldn't have done it, Captain," he said softly, "from your standpoint. But I know those Indians.

I knew it had to be done, and right then. Go ahead and arrest me. They're licked. That's what we wanted. You can have the glory. All I want to do is lie down and sleep for a month." He started to turn away. Forrester's words caught him up short.

"Butler."

He turned back. There was the same hard core of antagonism in Forrester's glance, but it was a little awry. His flat mouth was flatter and his body was just as erect. It was the sound of his voice that made Kit look at him. "Where's the girl?"

His eyes went flat and his mind reeled. Without answering or speaking at all, he turned his horse and kneed it back to where he had last seen her. With a depth of understanding Kit never would have attributed to the angry commanding officer, Forrester reined after him.

"Those mounted bucks broke through, Butler. Over there." He flung his arm out.

Kit looked along the field and saw dead horses. Two dead soldiers were sprawled grotesquely across the animals. His heart went dead within him. His mind got fuzzy.

"You know them. You know what they'll do if we go after them."

"Yeah." He reined up and shook his head, the way he had when Allie had insisted he was too tired to go on.

"Then think of something . . . quick!"

He dismounted near where she had been. The

ground offered an eloquent story in mute tragedy. The corporal and his guard had put up a gallant fight. They had been overwhelmed by force of numbers. The tracks led south, toward the forest. He got off his haunches and went back to stand by his horse, looking over where a heat haze obscured the glowering shadow world of trees. Forrester watched him in silence. He had seen much Indian ferocity but he had never gotten used to it, and never would. That, and the knowledge of what would happen to Allie Burgess, was prompting him, in spite of himself, to be lenient with the scout who had committed such an unpardonable breach of conduct—at least in the Army's eyes.

Kit mounted and rode in a tight little circle, quartering the path taken by the fleeing Dakotas. What he read from the earth confirmed what he already knew. They had been about fifteen strong. They had swept up the girl when they found her, and had taken her as a hostage.

He rode back toward the column. The men were sitting, eating and smoking, and drinking copious amounts of water. The sun was burnishing the valley with a blasting fury.

Captain Forrester dismounted when Kit did. He looked over at the Indians. Burial parties were at work. They had to grub in the earth with their hands and captured soldier sabers. The majority of the warriors were having a council.

Kit stood like a statue, staring at the Indians. He forced his mind to work with great effort. Thralldom—an emptiness—left him feeling weak and drained. Forrester walked over slowly and stood beside him.

"I hope they'll talk sense now, Mister Butler."

Kit got his idea from those eight words. He didn't move, though, until the officer spoke again.

"I'll ride out with a white flag and see."

"No." Kit turned and mounted his horse in a leap. He gathered the reins and stared at the officer. Bareheaded, the fullness of his mane in disarray, Captain Forrester looked younger.

"Well?"

"I've got a notion, Captain. I know the Army doesn't trade, but it's got to this time."

"What do you mean?"

"Trade them their lives for Miss Burgess."

Forrester continued his unblinking, squinted regard of the scout. He dropped his head a little and turned it, gazing out where the Indians were. "They're Army prisoners, one way or the other, Mister Butler," he said firmly, softly. "We can't let them walk away from here."

"Time's valuable," Kit said. "If we can save her at all, it's got to be done right now."

"We can't trade," Forrester repeated. "Not their freedom."

"It doesn't have to be their freedom. Trade them their lives."

"You mean butcher them if they don't have her sent back?"

"It wouldn't be the first time," Kit said. Then he shook his head. "No, I didn't mean that. I meant let them think that's what's going to happen to them."

"I don't follow you."

Kit let his shoulders droop. "Line up your men. Have them kneel and aim their guns. I'll ride ahead. I'll talk to them. When I lift my arm, you have them aim every gun at the Indians."

Forrester expelled his breath and started to shake his head. "This is no time to bluff," he said solemnly.

"This is exactly the time to bluff," Kit corrected him flatly. "It's the only time to bluff Dakotas. When you have the power and they think you have the will to carry through with it."

"I don't like it. Suppose some fool starts shooting?"

"Suppose we talk too long and they kill her?"

"How do you know they haven't already?"

"I don't, but I know them. As soon as the fighting ended, those mounted bucks found a high spot and are sitting up there, looking down. The rest is up to us. She's more valuable to them alive than dead . . . right now." Kit tightened his reins. The color came into his face. "Will you do as I'm asking?"

Forrester looked deeply troubled. He ran a hand

through his hair, then sheltered his eyes and stared out at the Dakotas. “You’re riding to your death, more than likely,” he said in a thin, resigned way. “All right. If hell breaks loose, you’ll be in the middle of it and we won’t be able to save you, Butler.”

Kit didn’t answer. He took off his hat and waved it in big, swooping motions, over his head, and began to ride slowly forward. Behind him, he could hear Forrester bellowing for his officers. Ahead of him, the Dakotas were standing up, a lot of them, staring. The bucks hunkering around the council turned and watched the lone white man riding his horse at a walk toward them. Several jumped up with shouts of rage. Others made the *wibluto* signal for sit-wait.

Kit could see the gesture very plainly. A balled fist held ear-high, then brought down sharply to shoulder height. Sit-wait. He stopped waving his hat and dumped it on the back of his head. His eyes burned with a fiery dryness and his body felt bruised as though from a physical pummeling.

A tall, handsome Dakota man of war arose very calmly, with great dignity, and walked forward through the watching warriors. Kit was conscious of the sudden hush that overhung the battlefield. Far back, over the heads of the Indians, he could see the crowd of small figures outside the wagon circle. They stayed very close, in case the Indians turned and threw themselves in desperation upon the only cover around them. He wondered where Lige was. Well, whatever happened, by nightfall the wagon train would be safe, anyway. There was a bitter shred of satisfaction in that thought until he recollected the faces of the Burgesses.

He winced and dropped his gaze to the Dakota warrior.

He had stopped, waiting Kit's advance, and was leaning on a dragoon carbine.

"*How-kola*."

The buck didn't respond. He stood, impassive and defiant, his black eyes swimming with rancor.

Kit dismounted and hunkered. The buck reluctantly dropped down. He kept the soldier gun clutched in both hands across his lap. "Where is White-Shield-Owner? I want to talk to him."

"He is dead."

That shook Kit. He flickered a glance to the thinned-out horde of warriors standing back, watching them. "Who is left?"

"Big Eagle is dead, also."

"*Owgh*! I knew them both very well. White-Shield-Owner was my old friend. I am sorry over him. My heart is on the ground."

"I am a lance bearer. I am the war leader now. I am Owl."

"I come to make a council with your warriors."

The war leader hesitated, then he got up and turned away. Kit walked beside him. As tall as Kit was, the Dakota was half a head taller. He led his horse and caught the scent of them once he was close. There was a feeling of deadliness around him almost instantly. He knew they knew who he was and that they hated him above all the other whites. He had outwitted them not once, but half a dozen times, and every time had come off triumphant.

Owl called the men of war. They came in bleak silence and dropped down. Kit waited until every man was hunkering, he himself standing, then he raised an arm and held it out before him, palm upward.

"I come to offer you peace. I come to offer you your lives. But I can't restrain the soldiers very long."

"Let them come," a scarred, older warrior said. He had a nose that had been badly broken some time and had healed crookedly so that, in the silence, the rasping, unpleasant sounds of his breathing were noticeable.

"They want to come," Kit said. "They want revenge. They want to wipe you out to a man, and they are strong enough to do it. They are twice as many as you are now. Behind you are the emigrants." He stopped and let it soak in before he spoke again.

"There are some of your friends up there in the forest. They were mounted. They left you."

"They couldn't reach us," Owl said calmly.

"It doesn't matter. The soldiers want to kill you. I have made talk for you."

"What kind of talk?"

"Like this. If you will throw down your weapons, you will be taken to Fort Collins and put in the stockade. You will not be massacred."

"It would be better to die!" the broken-nosed warrior said violently, gripping his bow until his dark hand was white.

"What about your villages? Do you want the babies and women to die, too? They will, if you don't get some wisdom."

"They might anyway," Owl said. "Who will look after them?"

"I will."

The older men looked beaten. One of them motioned Owl to silence with a weary, scrawny arm. "Your word is good. We know you, Ohiyesa. We are defeated."

"No!" the recalcitrant buck roared, shaking his bow at Kit and making as though to stand up. "I am no coward, no sheep to be herded into your white man stockade. I will . . ."

Kit raised his arm, took off his hat, and waved it. The other bucks turned and stared. The long, ominous blue line was a solid twinkling wall of aimed muskets. One man made a high, trilling sound of warning. The broken-nosed warrior twisted without moving and let his words trail off into thick silence.

Kit squatted then, and looked hard at the warriors. "There is one friend for you here. Me. I will be your friend and help you only if you will send two men to those warriors up in the trees to tell them to come down here and bring the girl they have stolen with them."

"A girl?" Owl asked, dumbfounded. "Where did they get a girl?"

"She was with the soldiers. I want her back here. If I don't get her back here before nightfall, I will turn my back on the Dakotas."

"If you do get her back," Owl asked. "What?"

"Then you will be prisoners of war. You will not be massacred. I will go to your villages and bring in your people. I will see that they are fed."

"And what of us?"

"I will promise you nothing. I cannot. You are the Army's prisoners."

"You are Ohiyesa to the Dakotas," Owl said strongly. "You are trusted by them. Will you swear to help us all that you can?"

"I will swear to that," Kit said firmly. Shrewdly he added: "For the sake of my dead brother, White-Shield-Owner."

"*Owgh*! It is the only way," an old warrior said with a glum look at the ground before his moccasined feet.

"*Owgh*!"

"*Owgh*!"

Kit listened, watching their faces. The only

actively reluctant one was the buck with the broken nose. He agreed because he had to, not because he wanted to. There were other recalcitrants, but the pointing guns from the heat-spanked line of blue kept their grumbling to a minimum.

Owl stood up and gazed at Kit. "It isn't much, Ohiyesa," he said.

Kit stood, also. "It can't be much. You have lost the battle."

"White-Shield-Owner and Big Eagle did that," the angry warrior said, with his twisted beak making the expulsion of his breath whistle. "They made us stay, even after the scouts said there were Comanches coming."

Kit looked at him with a dawning recollection. "Comanches?"

"Yes, the scouts who went after two who escaped from the wagon train ran into Comanches. One warrior was killed. The two whites got away. Maybe the Comanches got them."

Kit didn't enlighten the council about who the escapees were or how the Comanche sign came to be deep in their companion. The garrulous fighting man went on in his rumbling tone.

"They said we had to stay and conquer. That you . . . Ohiyesa . . . had stolen our horses and humbled the Dakotas. You . . . one man. You had to be taught your lesson. They made us stay. This was no good. Now . . ."

"Now it is over. But unless you agree to send for the girl and . . ."

"Send for her," the angry Dakota said with a disdaining gesture. "Send for her and herd us back like tame dogs. Take our land and our lives, our children and villages and . . ."

"No one will touch your villages or your children. They will be cared for." He turned swiftly toward Owl before anyone could break in upon him again. "Which are your two best travelers?"

"I will go," Owl said.

Kit shook his head. "No, you stay."

"You stay," the angry warrior said dourly. "They need a hostage, Owl. You must stay with your neck bowed."

"Be quiet!" Kit deliberately insulted the man. His nerves were raw and writhing. They exchanged a long, black stare, then Kit turned back to Owl. "Send two of your best runners. They can pick up the tracks where they went into the trees. There will be no other unshod horse marks there."

"You wait here," Owl said.

"No, I'm going back."

An old man whose body had a grass poultice tinted pink under a strip of blanket along his ribs nodded gravely. "Let him go, Owl."

No one objected. They seemed to settle into a deep lassitude, even the man with the broken nose. Their eyes hung on the ground with a dull luster.

Owl called out two names. Blue Crane and Red Soldier. These two were sent after the mounted Dakotas. Kit watched them lope away side-by-side, their bows held ready and their heads turned distrustfully toward the soldiers. He went over to his horse and swung up. The dejection of the proud Dakotas struck a compelling sympathy somewhere inside him. He looked at Owl.

"I will tell the soldiers everything will be all right. I will ride to the emigrant train and tell them they are not to shoot anymore."

No one spoke. He hadn't expected them to, and rode at a stiff trot back where Captain Forrester, his bullet-torn hat restored, was sitting on the ground in the shade of his horse, smoking a pipe.

"Did you pull it off?"

"Yes, at least they sent two runners to find the other bucks and bring them back."

Forrester said nothing. He made a mental reservation, however, regarding the fate of the mounted bucks, if they came back without their captive.

"I'm going over to the wagons."

"I'll come along."

"No, you'd better stay here. It might not be over yet."

Chapter Seventeen

Kit rode back across the no-man's land between soldiers and Dakotas, made a shambling circuit of the waiting Indians, busy with their wounds, their dead, and their final defeat, and headed down the land toward the wagons. He could hear them crying out his name long before he was close enough to identify any of them by appearance.

When he swung down and led his horse the last few hundred feet through the emigrants, questions flew as thick as the bullets had only shortly before. A strong hand gripped his sleeve finally, and stopped him. He looked over into the perpetually squinted, gray old eyes of Reuben Burgess.

"Where is she?"

He took Burgess's arm and led him along as he walked into the center of the circle. One swift glance showed the drawn, lean faces of the people and the tucked-up look of the animals. When they were a little apart, he dropped the older man's arm and faced him.

"The Indians captured her just after the fight started. Wait a minute! They've gone to get her . . . some other Indians. I think they'll fetch her back. I told them the Indians would be massacred if they didn't bring her back right away."

Burgess's face was the sick color of putty. The defiance and determination he had shown all through the ordeal was suddenly gone. He turned without another word and walked unsteadily toward his wagon. Kit started to go after him. A hand clawed at him. It was Lige.

"Dang! You're a sight for sore eyes."

"Where were you? I didn't see . . ."

"You won't believe it, maybe, but I fell asleep under a wagon just when your soldiers lit into 'em. I reckon a man can get too much unslept once in his life, anyway. Where's Allie?"

"They got her. I sent . . ."

"Damn!"

Kit wagged his head exasperatedly. "I think they'll bring her back all right, Lige."

"I'll fetch her back . . . damn their . . ."

"No, Lige!" He had to grab quickly. Lige was moving with more speed than Kit had seen him show in a long time. His face was working savagely. "Hold on, Lige."

"I'll . . . !"

"You'll do nothing. They've already sent two runners after her. They know their lives depend on her coming back unhurt."

"But how d'you know she ain't . . . hurt . . . already?"

"I don't, but there's a good chance of it. They aren't cannibals. It's the best way, Lige, the only way."

"How long'll it take 'em? By dawn, I could run 'em down in . . ."

"They ought to be back before sundown."

Lige canted his head at the sun. "Four, five hours." He looked harshly at Kit. "If she isn't back by then . . ."

"There'll be two of us, Lige. Now . . . how're things here?"

"We lost a few more. The day after you left, the Indians pulled out and didn't come back for two days."

"I know. I killed one that was trailing us and made up a fake Comanche arrow and stuck it in him."

"Oh, well, good for you. It gave us a breather. We didn't suffer too much, but if there hadn't been a creek running through this circle, we'd've been starved out."

"The horses don't look very good. How many more casualties?"

"Hell, the stock's suffered more'n we have. No grass left. Altogether we got about forty-two hurt, of which ten can't hold a gun. The rest of 'em's full of fight. We even had the womenfolk and that red-headed kid and his cronies under the wagons. It was a hold-off, Kit. All we had to do was keep 'em off, and pray." Lige made a dour face. "I'm no praying man, but I sure made up for the lost years this last five days, boy." He searched Kit's face with swollen eyes. "You run into anything much?"

"Nothing much, Lige. Just one little bunch that trailed us."

They didn't have another chance to talk for a long time. Kit was swamped with questions. The emigrants were elated at his success. The men were still full of brimstone, but the women cried. The sounds of their keening made a dismal background to the noises that were flooding outward from within the circle. But the time passed and Kit glanced often at the lowering sun. Lige and Reuben Burgess, sitting apart with his arm around the huddled shapelessness of his wife, alone knew what was lying black and heavy under Kit's heart.

The noise was distraction, and he needed it right then. Fear was growing. Lige's set face didn't leaven it any, that, and his growing quietness and the long, bitter way he would glance beyond the wagons at the huddling, completely surrounded Dakotas.

Then Kit heard the bugle again. He didn't know the call, but it brought his spirit up with a rush of fear and anguish. He walked toward a gap between wagons and leaned on the rough ash tongue that was lashed to the running gear of the wagon in front. His fingers bit deeply into the old wood, scoring it. He leaned there, waiting, seeing the deep red splash of sunlight on the strange circle with its motionless Indians inside.

There was a freighted silence, too, until Lige came over with too casual a step, and slouched, leaning against the oaken boot of the wagon, his swollen eyes fixed like stones, unmoving, with an awful intensity on the only thing that moved in all that vastness.

Horsemen and Indians were coming down out of the trees very slowly, riding as though they were reluctant to go out into the open country again. They were a long way off. Kit was straining every faculty to see them.

Lige pushed off the wagon and went stumping through the heavy dust. He wasn't gone long, and when he returned, he had a long brass spyglass in his hand. He worked the telescopic adjustment with fretting impatience and held it to his right eye, squinting. It was the sound of breath hissing past his tight lips that made Kit turn.

Lige lowered the glass without taking his eyes off the straggling cavalcade. "Here," he said, holding out the telescope. "Take a quick look."

Kit hoisted the glass and leaned back with his legs spread as though to receive a blow. The Indians were all out on the valley floor now. Their tired horses were shambling along, heads down and gaunt flanks rippling hollowly. The first two riders each had a second rider behind them, riding double. With unsteady hands Kit moved the glass slowly, studying each dejected, defeated man of war as he moved down the line. Then he saw her.

The black hair was loose, and even from that

distance with artificial aid he caught the deep blue sheen to it. He lowered the glass.

"Allie."

"Yeah," Lige said. "God bless her."

Kit handed back the spyglass and slumped down on the wagon tongue. "Lige, I'm going out there. Tell her folks, will you?"

"Be proud to, old-timer. See you when you fetch her back."

He watched Lige walk away before he stood up and started on weak legs for his horse. Swinging up, he waved away the people who would have detained him, rode out through the wagon circle, and made his circuitous way toward the knot of men by Captain Forrester.

The officer was smiling gently. All his earlier anger was gone. He shrugged to his feet, dusted his seat, and stood with one hand on Kit's horse's mane. "Go get her, Mister Butler. She'd like that better'n a soldier escort, I believe."

Chapter Eighteen

Kit rode to meet her. The Dakotas kept on riding toward the blue cordon, but they watched him closely. One called out a hollow greeting in a thick, tired voice. Kit returned it the same way, then he motioned them on toward the soldier line and swung in beside Allie. The girl's dress was torn again and her face was scratched from low-hanging limbs and spiny brush. Her eyes were swimming and smoky-looking.

"Your folks are all right, Allie."

She shook her head at him and blurted out a fast sentence: "I can't talk right now, Kit."

"I know," he said, reining far around the surround. "Let's go this way. It'll give you time to get set to see 'em, Allie."

They rode slowly around the soldiers and ignored the curious, steady stares they got. Back at the wagons a great shout went up. It carried far. Kit rode through the emigrants to the Burgess wagon and handed her up to her father. He dismounted and waved the people away, and led his animal past the throng with a shake of his head at every question. He found Lige and told him not to let any of them annoy the reunited family.

She needed time. He knew that. At the break in the circle he remounted and sat there slumped, looking back. The emigrants were in a festive mood. The women were scurrying between the old wagons and the cooking holes. The men and boys were talking too loudly. The strain seemed to have vanished like mist from their grimed, drum-tight faces.

He rode steadily across the trampled grass toward the Indians. From far across the circle he saw Forrester coming, too. There were four soldiers with the officer. They met where Owl and his tragic-faced warriors were watching them approach balefully. Some of the bucks were chewing pemmican and *wasna*. Kit dismounted and dropped down among them without a word. As though he wasn't there at all, the Dakotas went on eating and looking at the ground.

When Captain Forrester dismounted, he clanked with metal. The Indians swallowed with difficulty at the sound. Kit thought, too, it had an echo of chains to it.

To Kit's surprise Forrester knew *wibluto*, sit-wait. He knew it very well, too. Kit's respect for the soldier climbed. Without any preliminaries Forrester started to address the Dakotas. He told them they were strong men of war. He said their hearts were strong and his own heart was good toward them. He then asked them what Kit had promised them in return for the girl.

Owl started to speak in Dakota. Forrester frowned and made the Indian sign for deafness.

He didn't understand the tongue. Owl switched over to sign talk. Kit watched closely. The young warrior explained everything exactly as it was. Forrester looked at Kit with raised eyebrows. Kit nodded.

"That's exactly what I told them."

Forrester nodded. "All right. That's easy enough. We'd do that much anyway."

Owl was looking straight at Kit. "Can we camp here for tonight, or do we have to start the Long Walk now?"

Kit asked Forrester. The officer said they might stay if they gave him their word they wouldn't try to escape in the darkness. It was a weak stipulation, and they all knew it. If the Army had tried to herd them through the pass in the darkness, they would have lost them all, anyway.

"You can stay," Kit said. "We will march at dawn." He understood why Owl wanted to wait. "Where is your *hayoka*?"

"He is dead," Owl said, "but we have a strong medicine man still alive."

Kit stood up stiffly. "You have my word," he said to the council in Dakota. "My heart is good. I am still your friend and your brother. I will work for you. Trust me."

"*Owgh*!"

"*Owgh*!"

Even the vanquished warrior with the broken nose grunted belief and approval.

Forrester stood, then walked around to Kit, and offered his hand. "There was one time today that I could have shot you, Mister Butler," he said.

"The name's Kit."

"Kit, then. But I've got a bad fault. I can see both sides too easily, sometimes. I understood how you felt when you did that. We won, anyway. That's what counts, isn't it?"

Kit gripped the hard, bony hand and nodded. "I reckon so, Captain." Kit was embarrassed. "Shall I move the train out at dawn?"

"Yes, we'll make a dry camp and keep every man to horse all night. I don't believe they'll try anything . . . but I'm no gambler, either."

Kit dropped Forrester's hand. "We'll put the bells on the teams when we're ready to move out, then. See you tomorrow."

He rode back into the circle just before darkness fell. The emigrants were laughing and shouting. The sounds were strange to him. He turned his horse loose and sought Lige.

"Pardner, you keeled over asleep, you said. Well, I'm going to, right now."

"Fair enough," Lige said with a hard grin. "Take that wagon yonder. I already put your stuff in it."

"Good. Lige, break the camp at dawn and have 'em put on the team bells if I'm not awake by then."

"All right," Lige said, looking up into the

sunken eyes. "Allie sent you word she wants to thank you, Kit."

"It'll keep."

He went to the wagon, sprang over the tailgate, found a soft place, burrowed low, and didn't even bother to take off his hat or boots.

At dawn Lige lined them out. Every team and span of oxen had yoke and collar bells on them. They made a festive, joyous sound and it couldn't have been more appropriate, either, although the purpose had nothing to do with the exuberance and thankfulness of the people. The bells were to let each wagoner know how far ahead and how far behind each wagon was, when they got into the gap up ahead. This eliminated a lot of riding back and forth and served to let each drover know what the distance ahead and behind was.

The soldiers didn't herd the Dakotas. Some of the Indians were given horses to ride, but most of them walked. At Lige's grim suggestion, they were kept up with the Army and not allowed to drop back where the emigrants were.

The animals were hard to handle because of their recent starvation, so an early nooning was made. After that, they made good time and hit the gap in the late afternoon and kept right on going, their bells ringing, their animals strong and willing, and the people silent with gratefulness.

Kit awakened late in the afternoon. He caught Lige riding by, and sent him after a razor. Shaving and washing inside the lurching, rumbling Conestoga was no mean feat, but he accomplished it. Then he was fed by the solicitous people who owned the wagon, and Lige brought his horse up, saddled and bridled. He mounted it and rode beside Lige for an hour. They talked of a hundred things, and when the conversation lagged, Kit rode over to the Burgess wagon as though drawn by a magnet.

Allie was riding a horse, astride. She watched him swing around her parents' vehicle, and smiled at him. She looked freshly scrubbed. Except for the stillness in the background of her eyes and the leaner, more mature look to her face, she was exactly as the picture in his heart showed her.

"Feel better, Kit?"

"Lots better. I even took a bath."

"You look a lot better without the whiskers."

"You're a picture yourself, Allie. Prettiest picture in the West."

She flushed, and her gray eyes sparkled. He turned and gazed up at the towering spires on each side of the pass. "How'd you like to ride up there?" he asked, without looking around at her.

"I'd love to. Is there a way?" She, too, was studying the purple monoliths with a hushed look.

"Yes, there's a trail I used to use when we trapped this country. Come on, I'll show you."

She followed him far down the wagon train at a

lope. He wasn't conscious of the eyes that followed them, but she was. Where the southern slope of the bisected crags hunched low on the valley floor, he found the old trail and started up it. She followed behind him with high color in her face.

They plodded upward until they came to a sentinel clearing where the great, warm strokes of the sun's blood-red paint were lavished on the sere, wind-swept space, and there he dismounted and helped her down. Up here, high above the wagons, with just the faintest echo of the team bells coming very, very faintly, the quiet was louder than any noise could have been.

She stood looking out over the race of landfall southward, then down where the big old wagons were creaking and lumbering, as small as little animals. She turned and looked at his profile. "Is this where the Sioux sentries were?"

"Yes." He smiled gently back at her. "This is also a place where their medicine men come to pray. It's a sacred spot. They're pretty close to God up here, at that." Embarrassed at what he'd said, he turned away and looked with a brooding expression, northward. The jumble of mountains and forests and broad, green valleys ran out to the limits of the world and merged with the paling horizon.

"You never talked about God before, Kit."

"No," he said slowly, without looking away

from Dakota country. "Lots of men don't. That doesn't mean they don't talk to Him, Allie. Places like this are churches to me."

She dropped down on the barren knob and looked up at his lean, weary face. "Sit here, Kit, beside me."

For a long time neither of them spoke, then Kit raised his arm and pointed with a little twig he was holding between his fingers. "See that black-looking mountain over yonder, the one with the pinch of snow still on it?"

"Yes." But she didn't look at it very long. His face held her attention fully.

"That's what the Dakotas call the Mountain Monastery. You go up there to seek visions and talk to God."

"Have you ever been up there?"

"Yes."

"Seeking a vision?"

His arm dropped and the little twig made a scratching sound against the stony ground. "No, to talk to God. Once, about five years ago, I went on a vision quest. I don't believe white men have much success there. Maybe they don't believe . . . I don't know . . . but I didn't get any vision. Just cussed near froze to death." He turned to her with a wry smile. "That's one Indian trick I don't put too much faith in."

"Kit, you love this country, don't you?"

"Yes. I've traveled around quite a little, Allie.

I always come back here. I reckon I'll die here."

"Is that why we rode up here?" she asked with rare insight, looking at him steadily with her smoky-eyed gaze.

He nodded. "Yes, Allie, you're going on, but I belong here. I'd never be any good as a farmer. Maybe I believe like the Indians do. I don't want to plow a big wound in the breast of my mother, the earth." He twisted the little stick between his fingers. "I love you, Allie. I want you to know that. But maybe it'd be better if I didn't. I don't know. Anyway, I'll never forget you, Allie. Never."

She looked for a long time into the failing light before she said anything, then her voice was low. "No, Kit. I'm not going on. I told my folks. Dad understands."

"Told them what?"

"That this is your country, that you'd never be happy anywhere else." She looked at him quickly. "I knew that, Kit. I've always known it. Don't ask me how I knew. It was a dozen things. The way you feel about the Indians, the way you know every trail. It all came to the same thing. This is Kit Butler's country. I knew it right from the start. A woman who loves a man like you, I suppose, has to adjust, Kit, and make herself understand things like this." She looked down at the crawling wagons. "I'm not going any farther than Fort Collins, Kit."

He put down the stick and looked at Allie. There

was nothing said for several moments, and the wagon bells were fainter. He arose abruptly and walked over to where he could see the sun curling around the distant landfall beyond the pass.

"How do you know you'll be happy here, Allie?"

She walked up behind him. "Because you'll be here. That's enough."

He whirled. "Is it? Are you sure?"

"As sure as any woman ever was, Kit."

He didn't reach for her, just felt for her hand, and drew her up beside him where they could both see the distance and the little worms that were Conestogas, breaking out into the sun-splashed plain beyond the pass. They stood there, looking westward before she broke the lingering, hurting silence.

"I need you, Kit," she said in a small voice.

"Allie."

"Let me tell you something else, too. You're a great man. You'll see pretty soon. I'll be terribly proud of you one of these days, Kit. I didn't understand you before. None of us did. We do now. Even my mother and father do. You'll be a big man when this country comes of age. I'll be proud of you. So will our children, Kit."

He squeezed her hand and looked down at her with an embarrassed little wisp of a smile. "I reckon, then, we're going to get married."

"Yes," she said.

Then he kissed her.

About the Author

Lauran Paine who, under his own name and various pseudonyms has written over a thousand books, was born in Duluth, Minnesota. His family moved to California when he was at a young age and his apprenticeship as a Western writer came about through the years he spent in the livestock trade, rodeos, and even motion pictures where he served as an extra because of his expert horsemanship in several films starring movie cowboy Johnny Mack Brown. In the late 1930s, Paine trapped wild horses in northern Arizona and even, for a time, worked as a professional farrier. Paine came to know the Old West through the eyes of many who had been born in the 19th Century, and he learned that Western life had been very different from the way it was portrayed on the screen. "I knew men who had killed other men," he later recalled. "But they were the exceptions. Prior to and during the Depression, people were just too busy eking out an existence to indulge in Saturday-night brawls." He served in the U.S. Navy in the Second World War and began writing for Western pulp magazines following his discharge. It is interesting to note that all of his earliest novels (written under his own name and the pseudonym Mark Carrel) were published in the British market and he soon had as strong a following in that country as in the United States. Paine's Western fiction is characterized by strong plots, authenticity, an apparently effortless ability to construct situation and character, and a preference for building his stories upon a solid foundation of historical fact. *Adobe Empire* (1956), one of his best novels, is a fictionalized account of the last twenty years in the life of trader William Bent and, in an off-trail way, has a melancholy, bittersweet texture that is not easily forgotten. In later novels like *The White Bird* (1997) and *Cache Cañon* (1998), he showed that the special magic and power of his stories and characters had only matured along with his basic themes of changing times, changing attitudes, learning from experience, respecting Nature, and the yearning for a simpler, more moderate way of life.

Center Point Large Print
600 Brooks Road / PO Box 1
Thorndike, ME 04986-0001 USA

(207) 568-3717

US & Canada:
1 800 929-9108
www.centerpointlargeprint.com